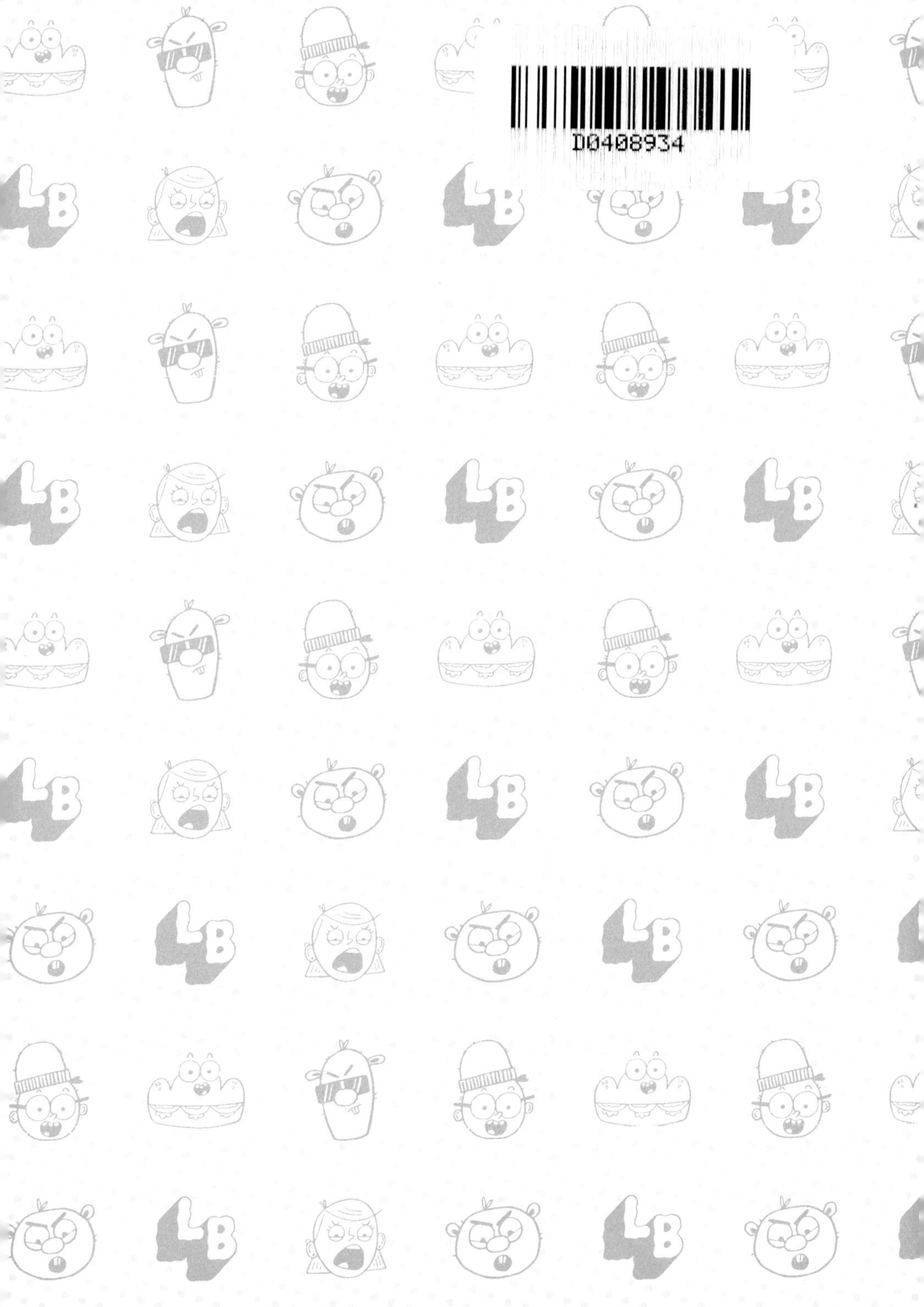

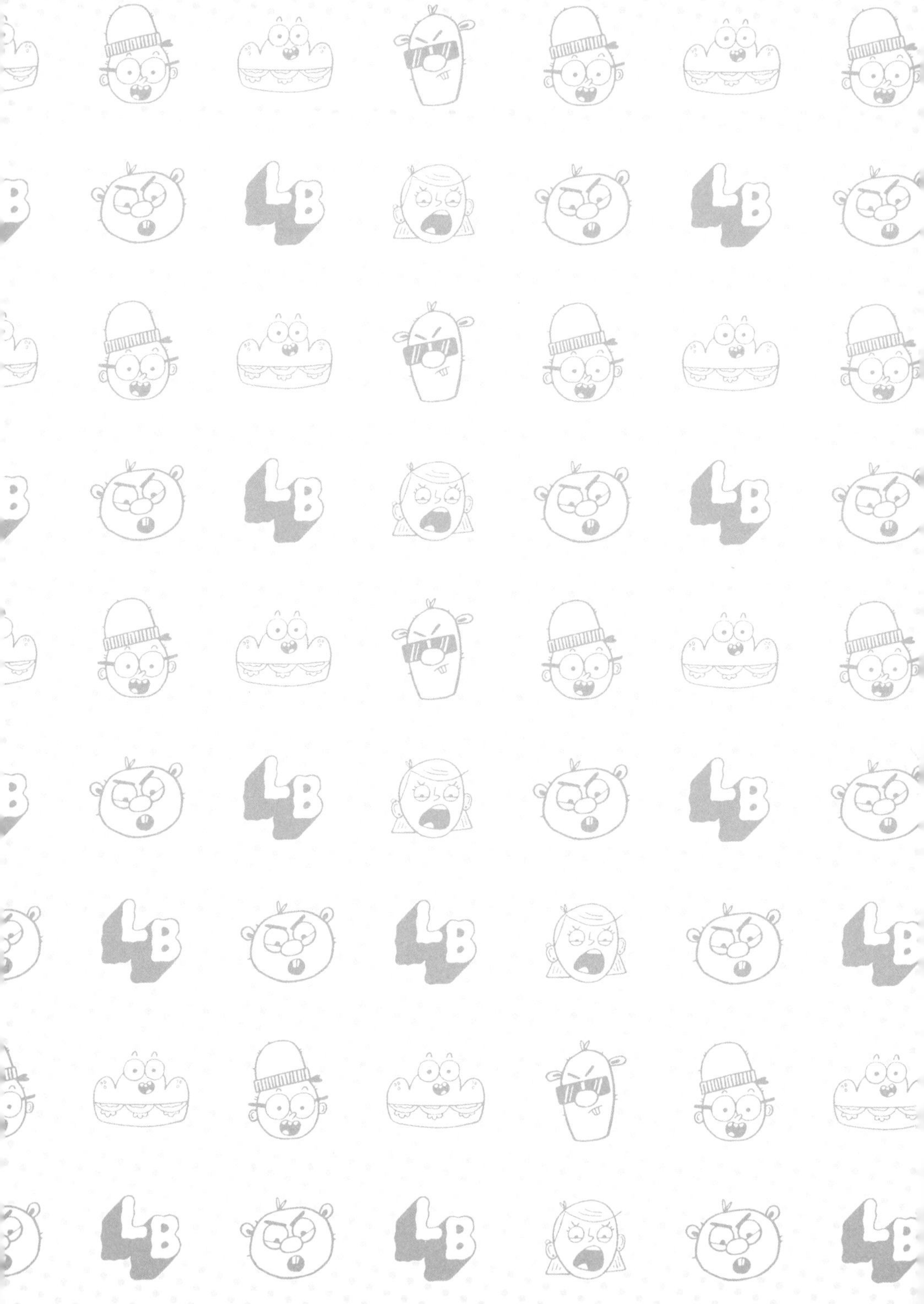

LUNCH BUDDIES

Battle in the Backyard

SMELLY SAM'S
SUPER
SPECIAL
SANDWICH
SAUCE

Daniel Wiseman

HARPER
alley

An Imprint of HarperCollinsPublishers

For Henry, Hugo, and River

HarperAlley is an imprint of HarperCollins Publishers.

Lunch Buddies: Battle in the Backyard
Copyright © 2023 by Daniel Wiseman
All rights reserved. Manufactured in Bosnia and Herzegovina.
No part of this book may be used or reproduced in any manner
whatsoever without written permission except in the case of brief
quotations embodied in critical articles and reviews.
For information address HarperCollins Children's Books, a division
of HarperCollins Publishers, 195 Broadway, New York, NY 10007.
www.harperalley.com

Library of Congress Control Number: 2023933190
ISBN 978-0-06-323623-3 (hardcover) — 978-0-06-323622-6 (pbk.)

This book was illustrated using Photoshop and caffeine.
Typography by Daniel Wiseman and Andrew Arnold
23 24 25 26 27   GPS   10 9 8 7 6 5 4 3 2 1

First Edition

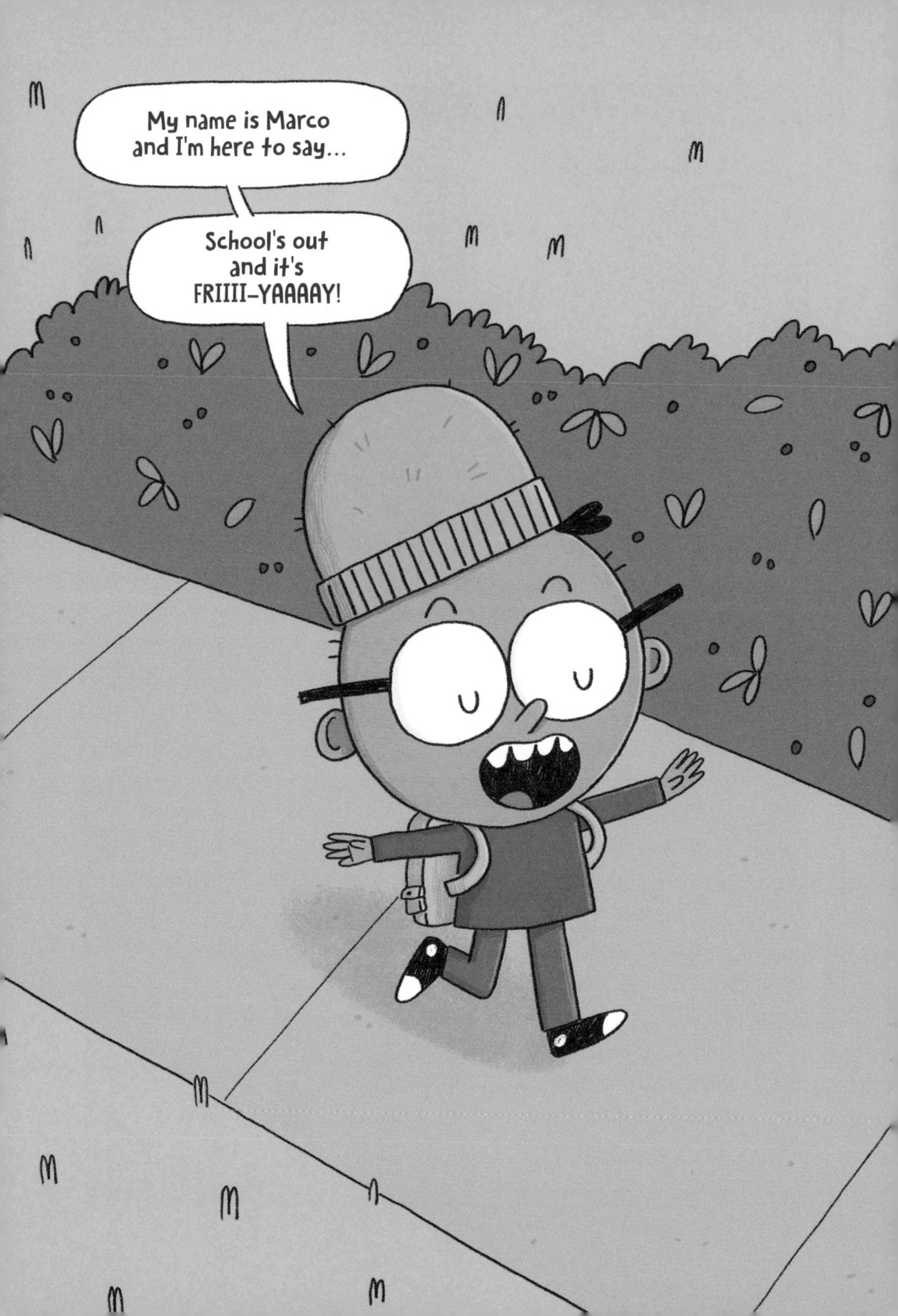
My name is Marco and I'm here to say...
School's out and it's FRIIII-YAAAAY!

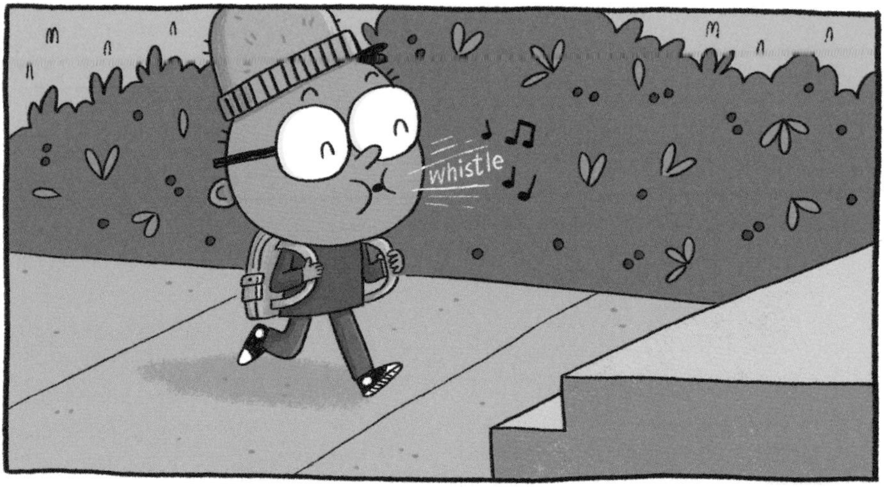
whistle

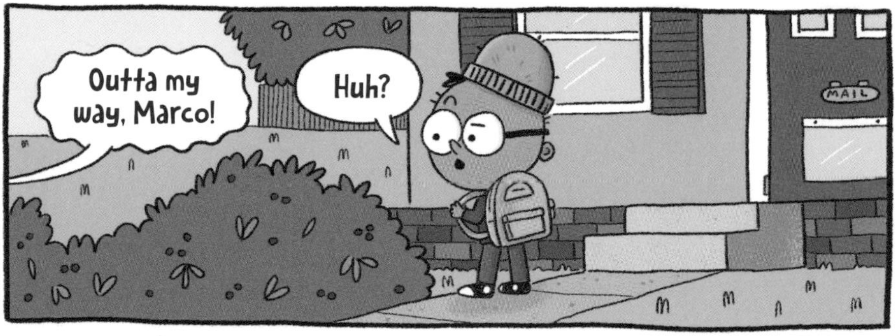
Outta my way, Marco!
Huh?
MAIL

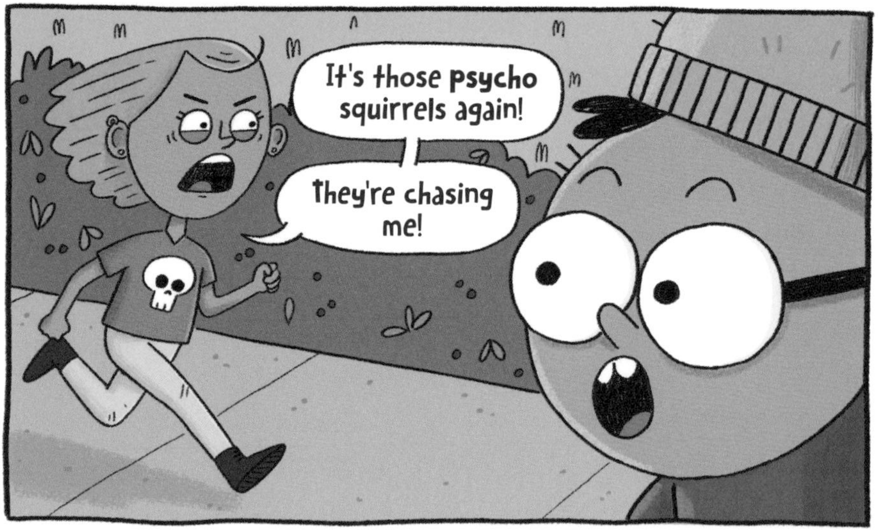
It's those psycho squirrels again!
They're chasing me!

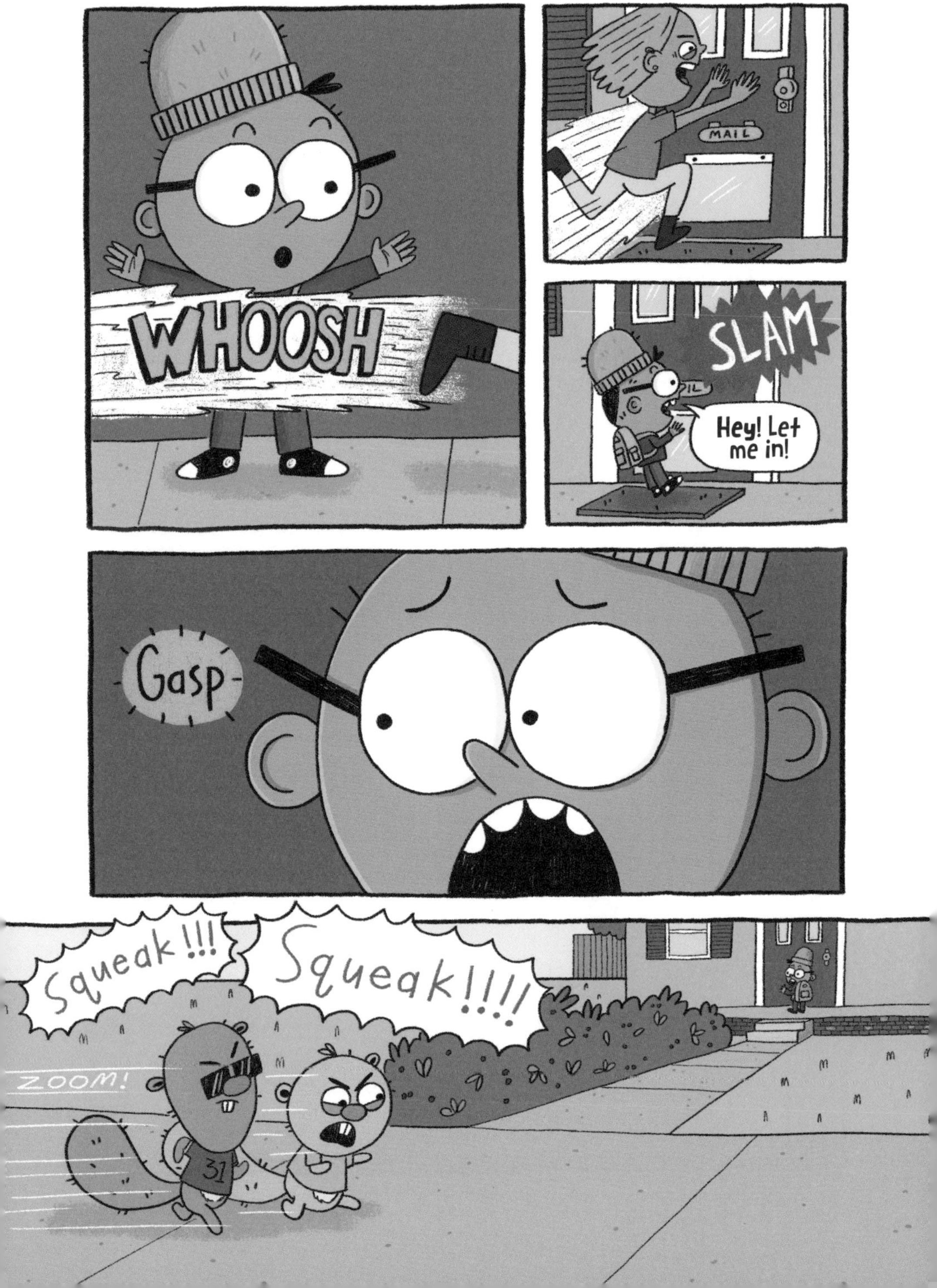
WHOOSH
MAIL
SLAM
Hey! Let me in!
Gasp
Squeak!!!
Squeak!!!!
ZOOM!
31

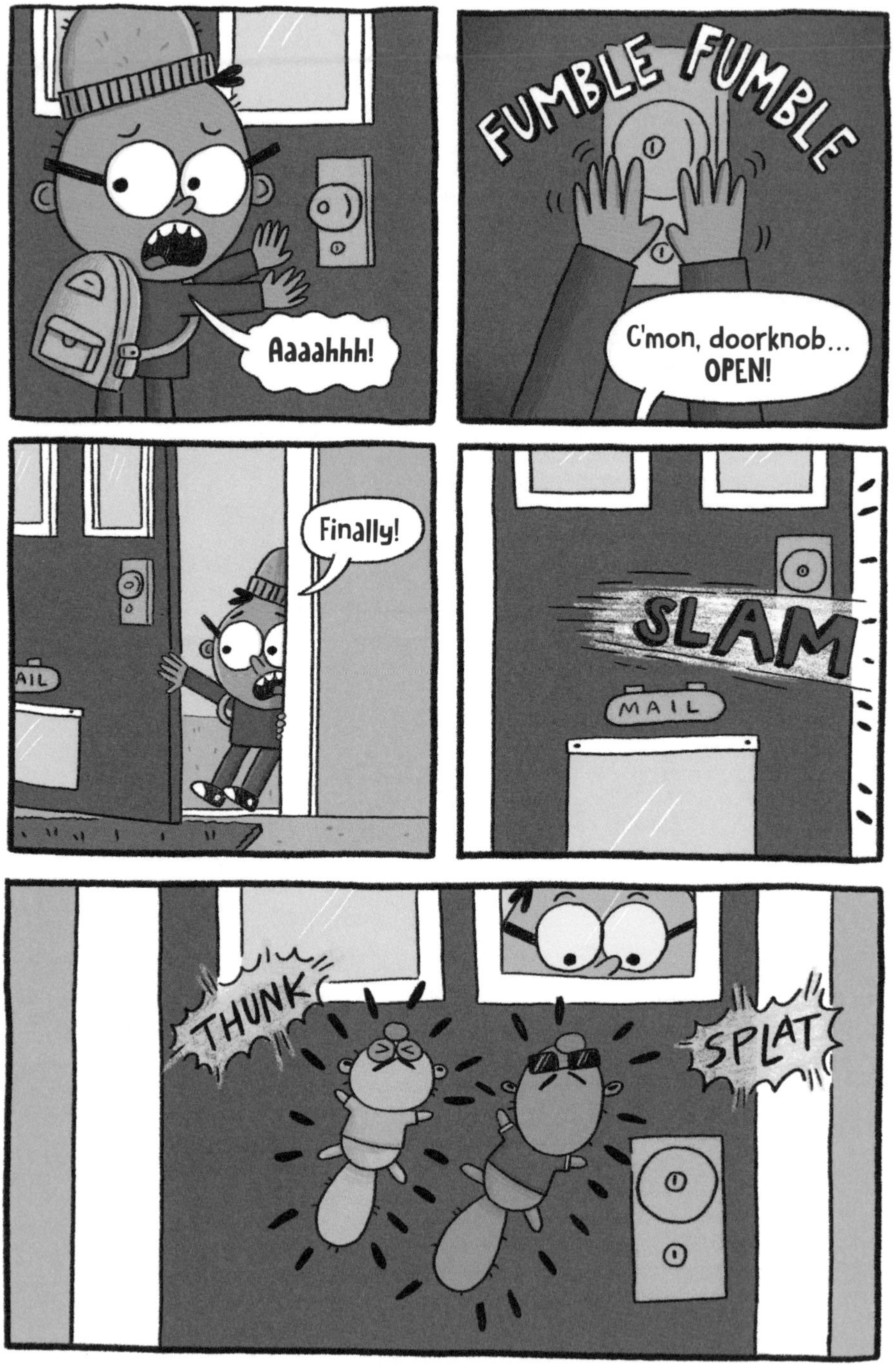
Aaaahhh!
FUMBLE FUMBLE
C'mon, doorknob... OPEN!
Finally!
SLAM
MAIL
THUNK
SPLAT

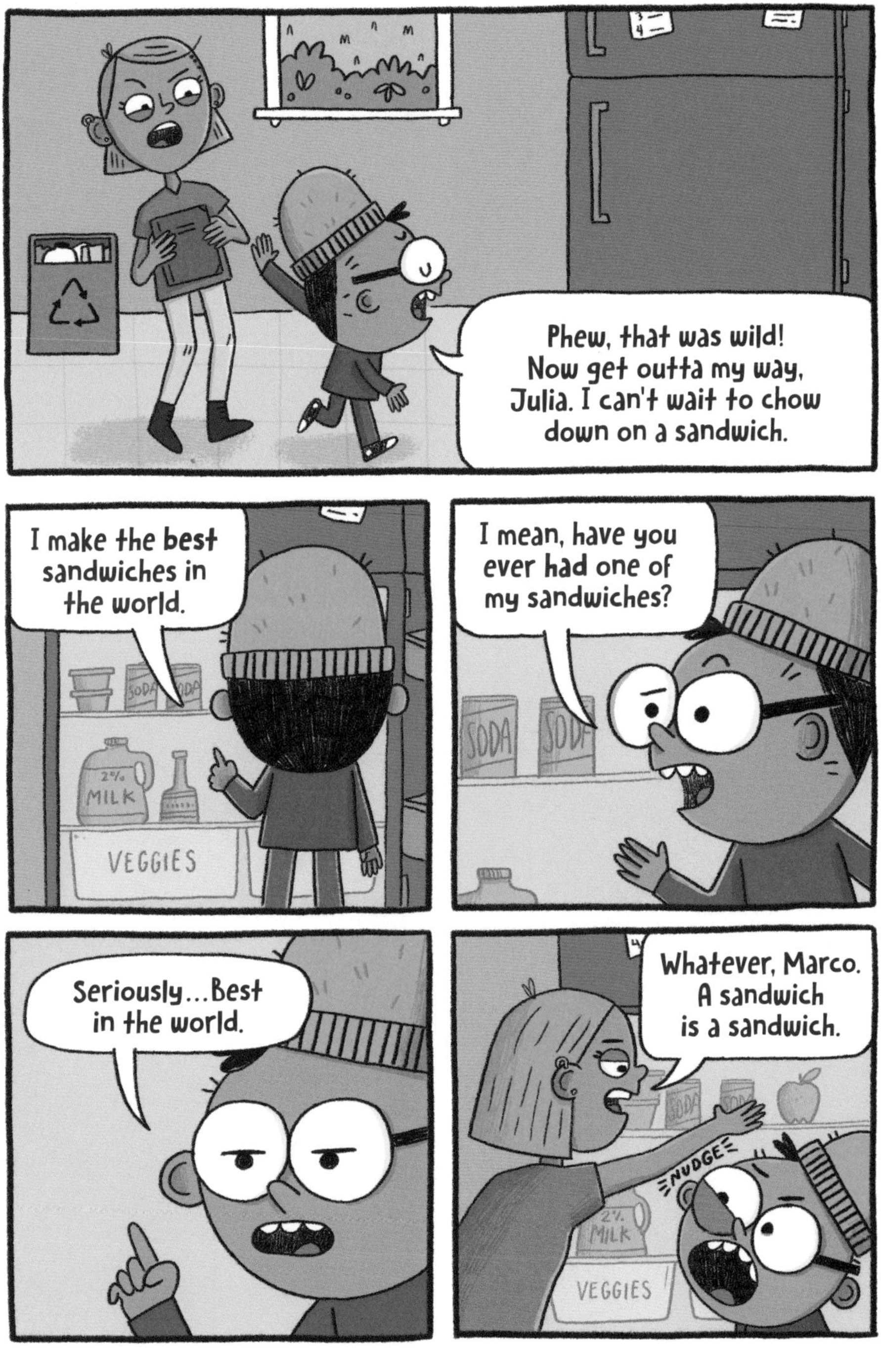
Phew, that was wild! Now get outta my way, Julia. I can't wait to chow down on a sandwich.
I make the best sandwiches in the world.
SODA
SODA
2%
MILK
VEGGIES
I mean, have you ever had one of my sandwiches?
SODA
Seriously...Best in the world.
Whatever, Marco. A sandwich is a sandwich.
NUDGE
2%
MILK
VEGGIES

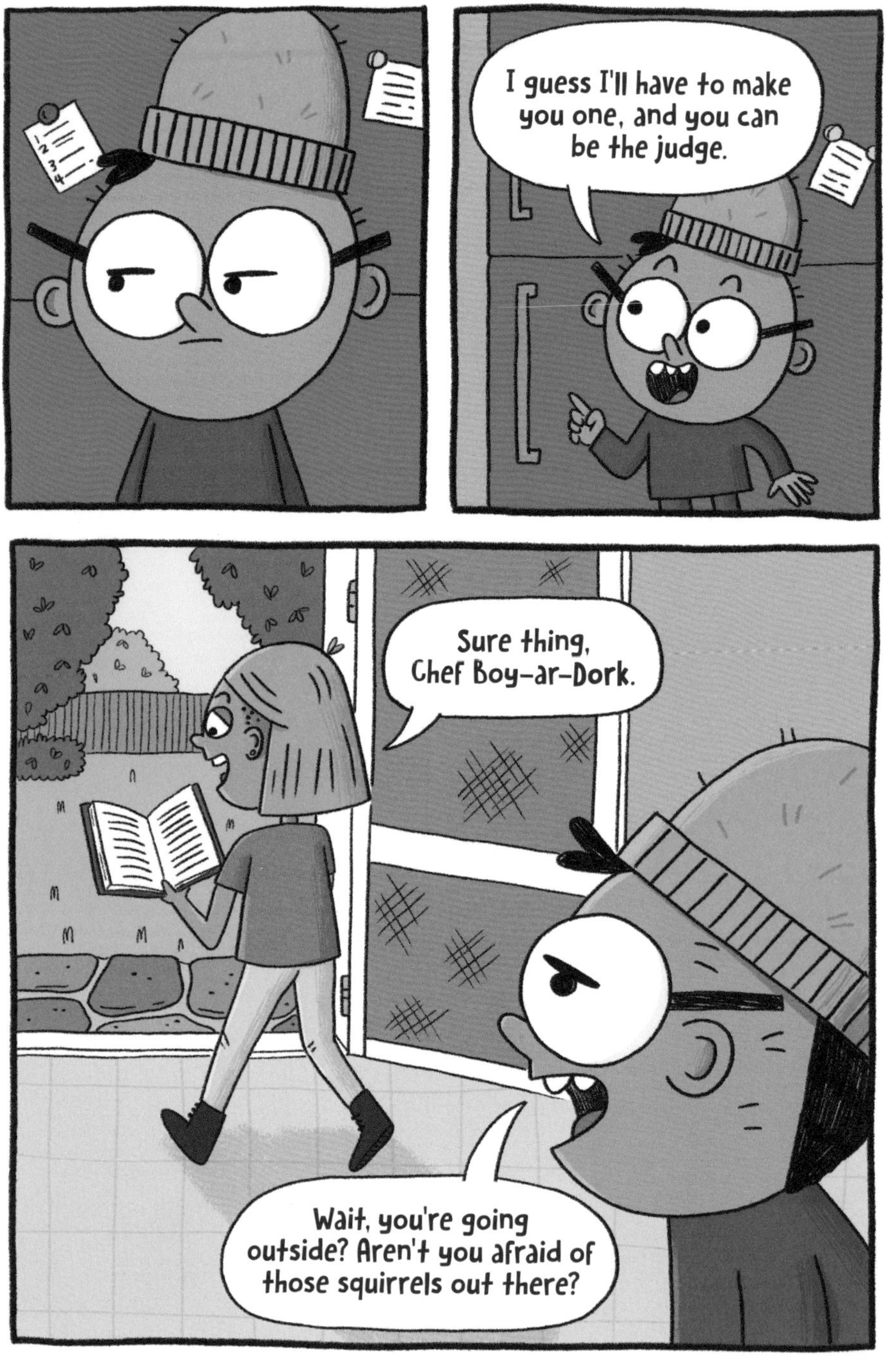
I guess I'll have to make you one, and you can be the judge.
Sure thing, Chef Boy-ar-Dork.
Wait, you're going outside? Aren't you afraid of those squirrels out there?

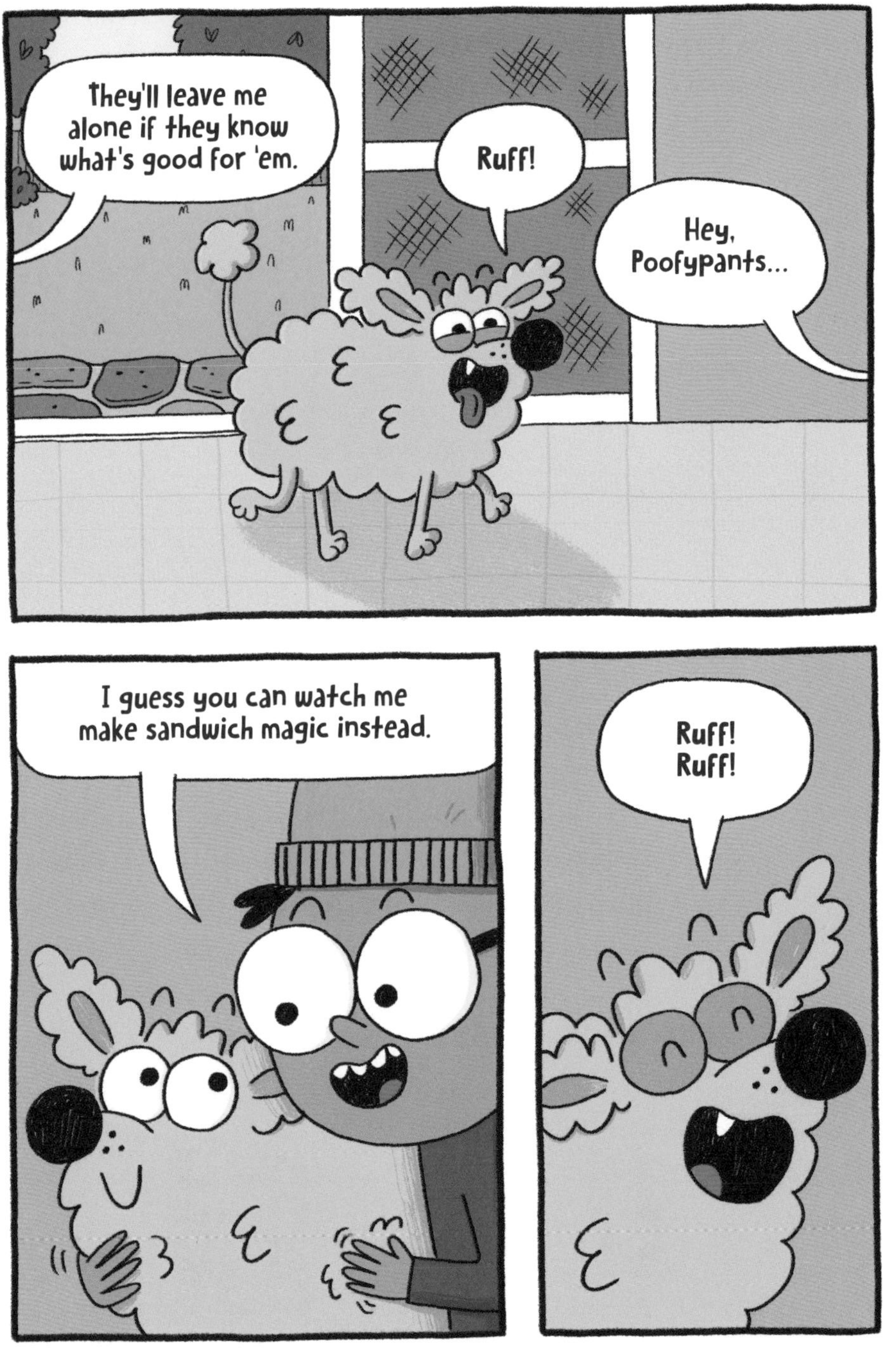
They'll leave me alone if they know what's good for 'em.
Ruff!
Hey, Poofypants...
I guess you can watch me make sandwich magic instead.
Ruff! Ruff!

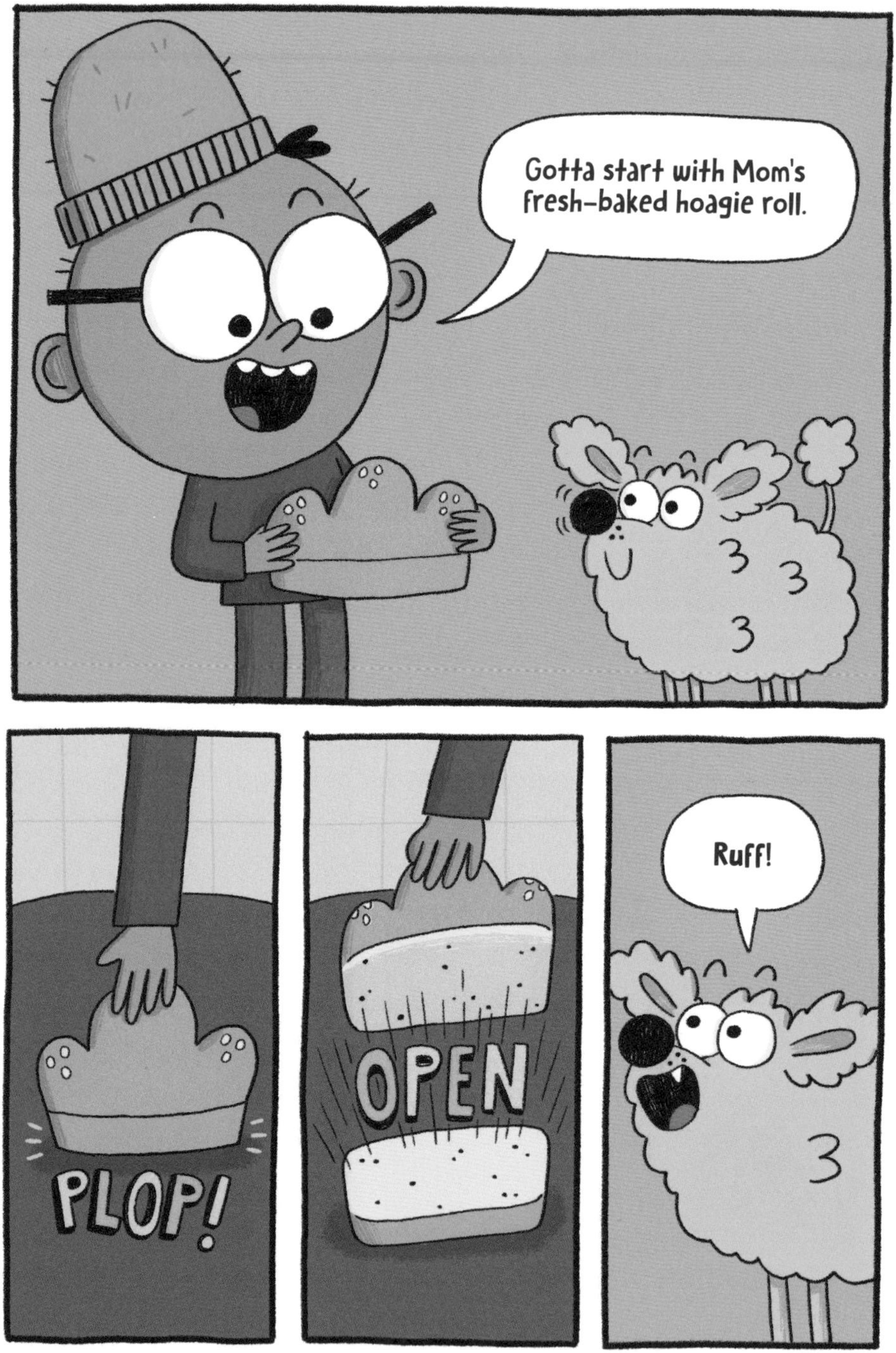
Gotta start with Mom's fresh-baked hoagie roll.
PLOP!
OPEN
Ruff!

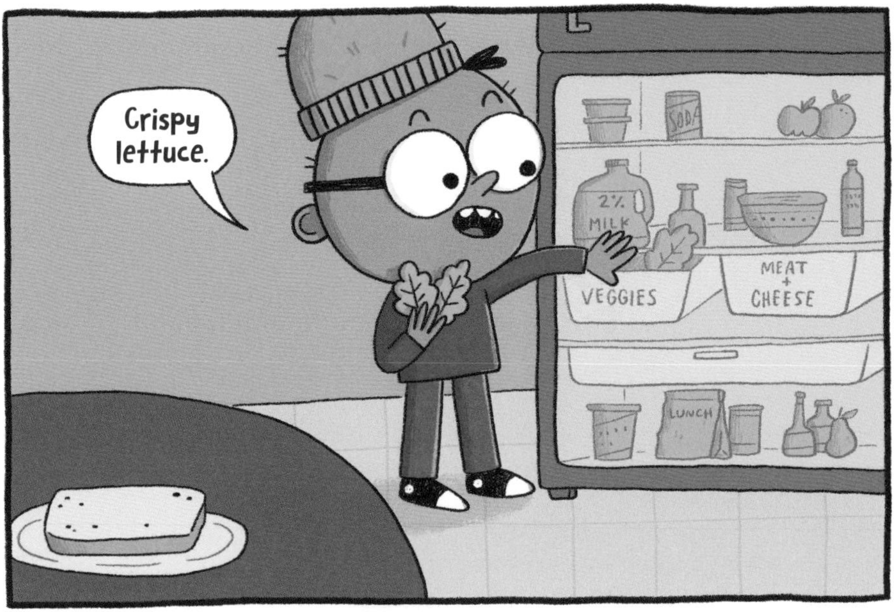
Crispy lettuce.
SODA
2% MILK
VEGGIES
MEAT + CHEESE
LUNCH

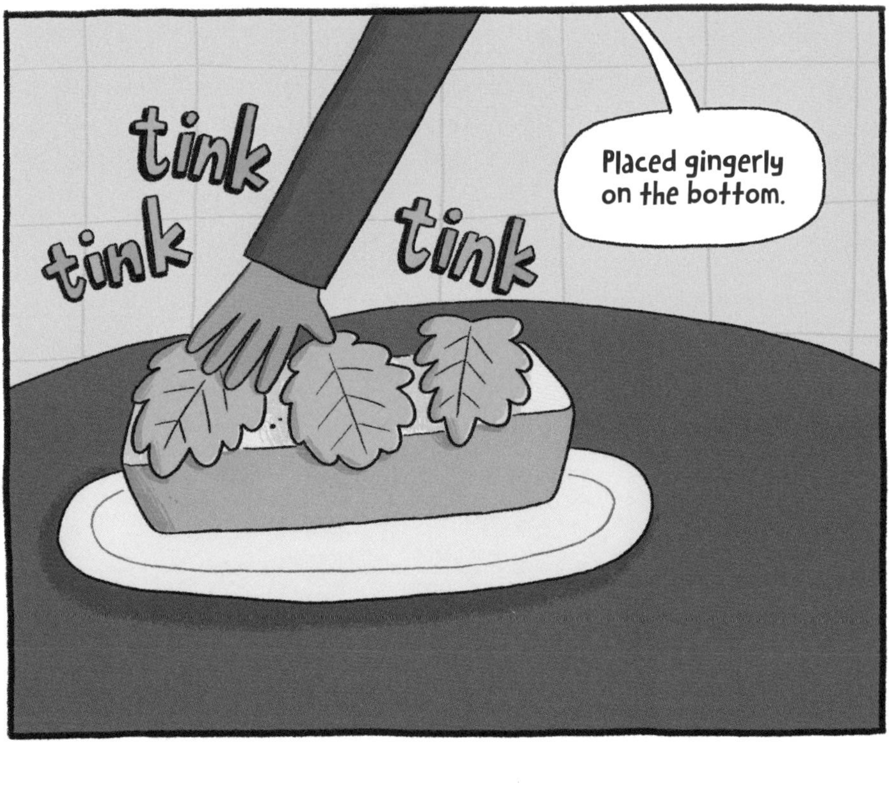
Placed gingerly on the bottom.
tink
tink
tink

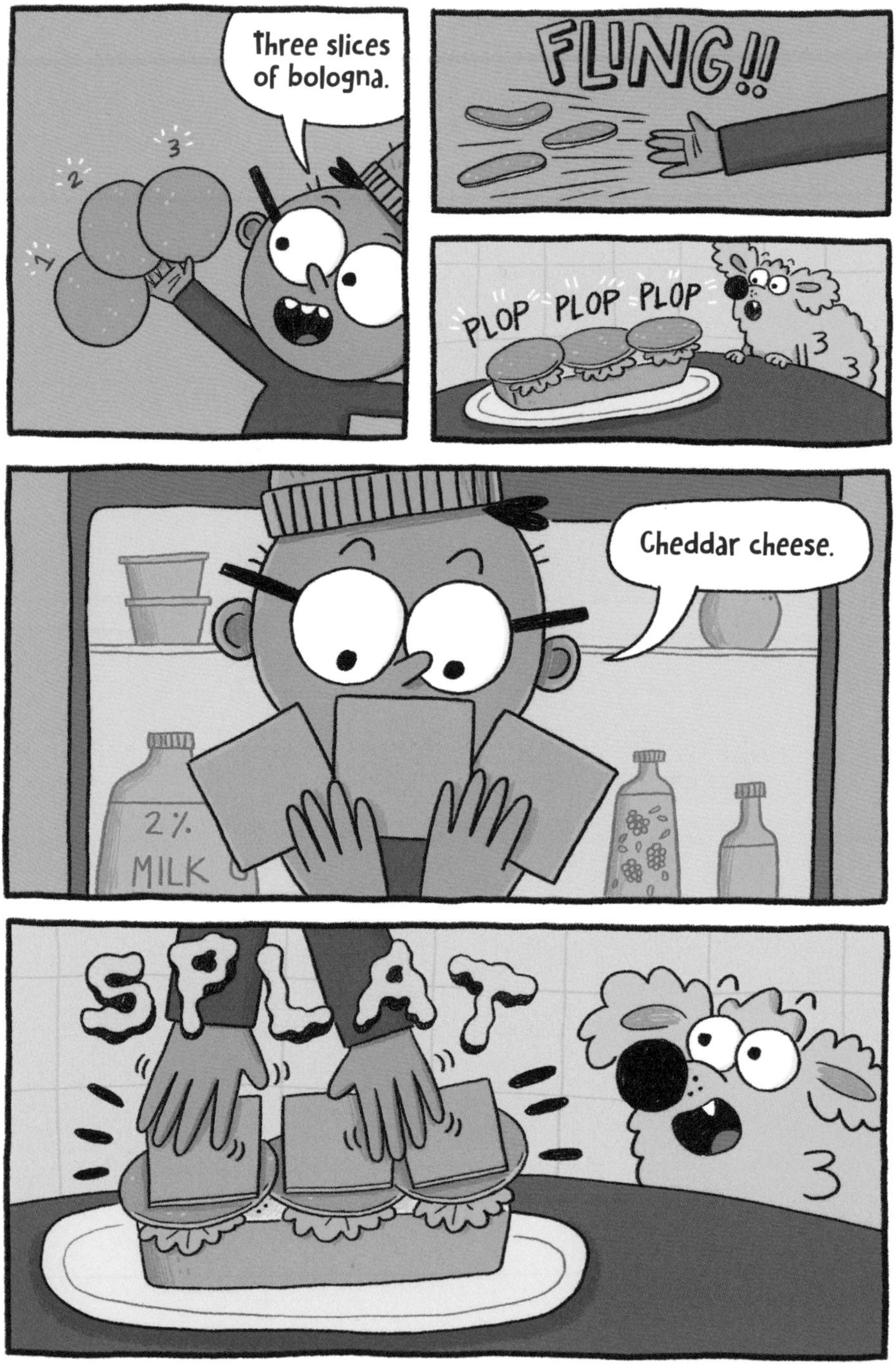
Three slices of bologna.
1
2
3
FLING!!
PLOP PLOP PLOP
Cheddar cheese.
2%
MILK
SPLAT

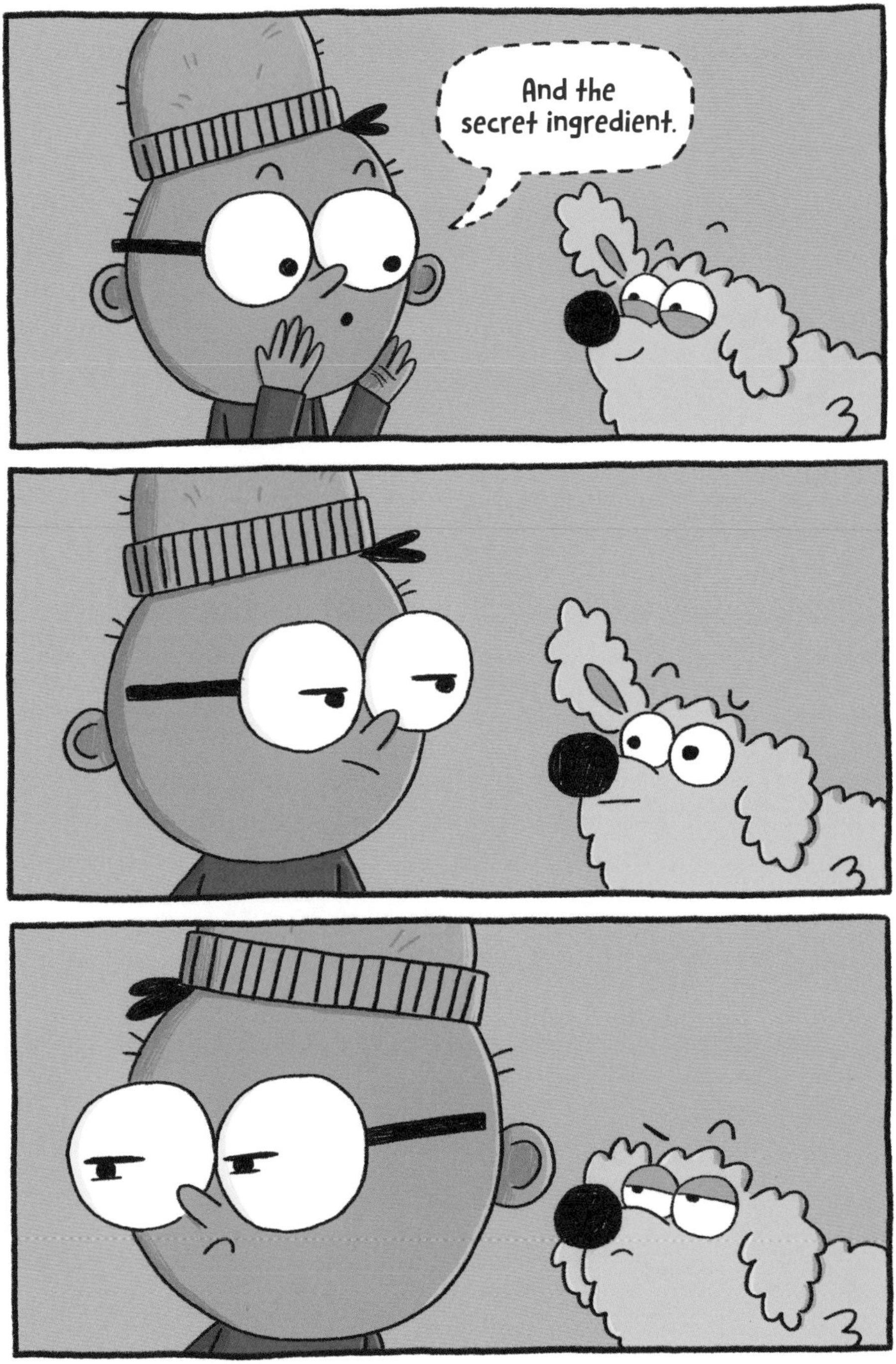
And the secret ingredient.

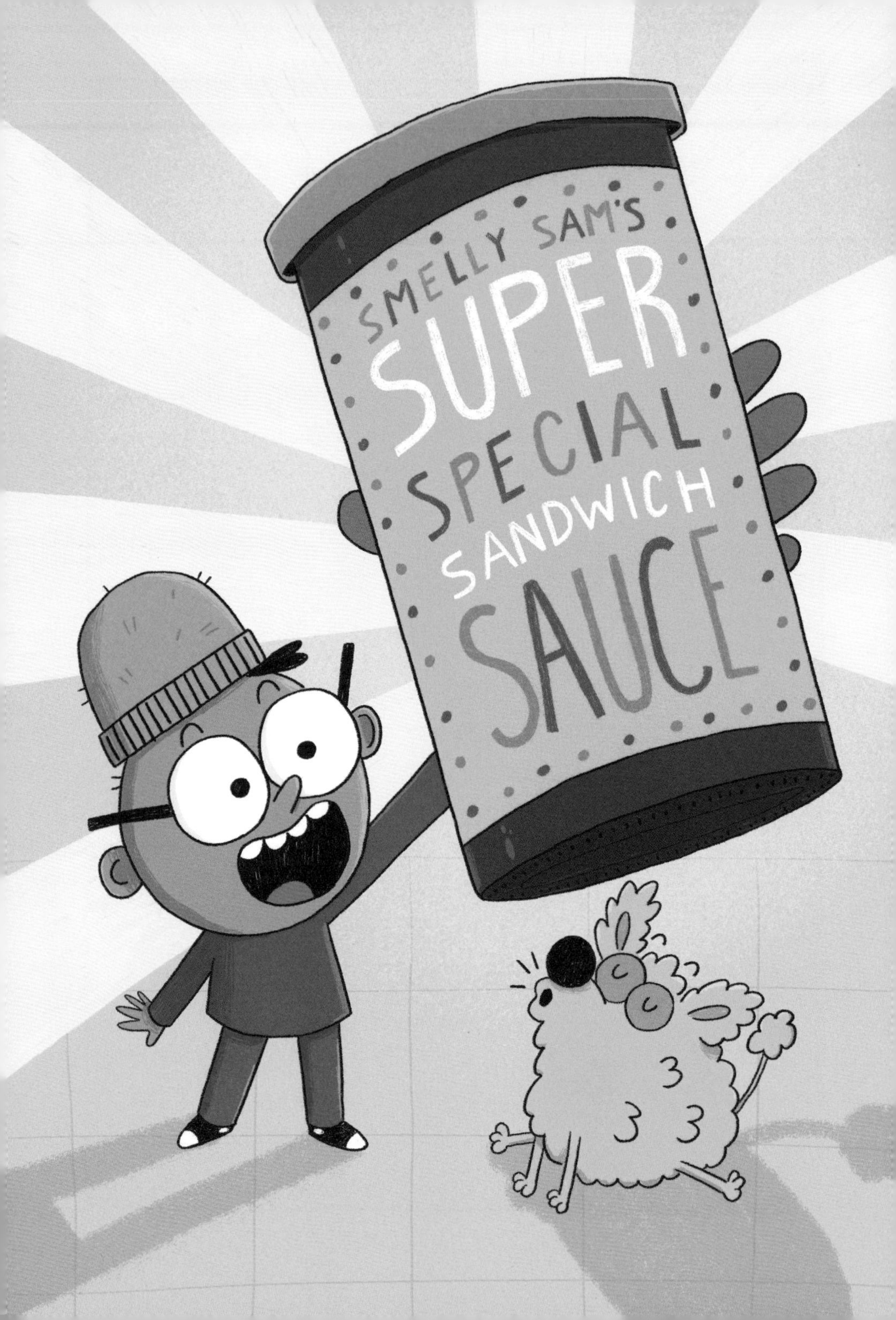
SMELLY SAM'S
SUPER
SPECIAL
SANDWICH
SAUCE

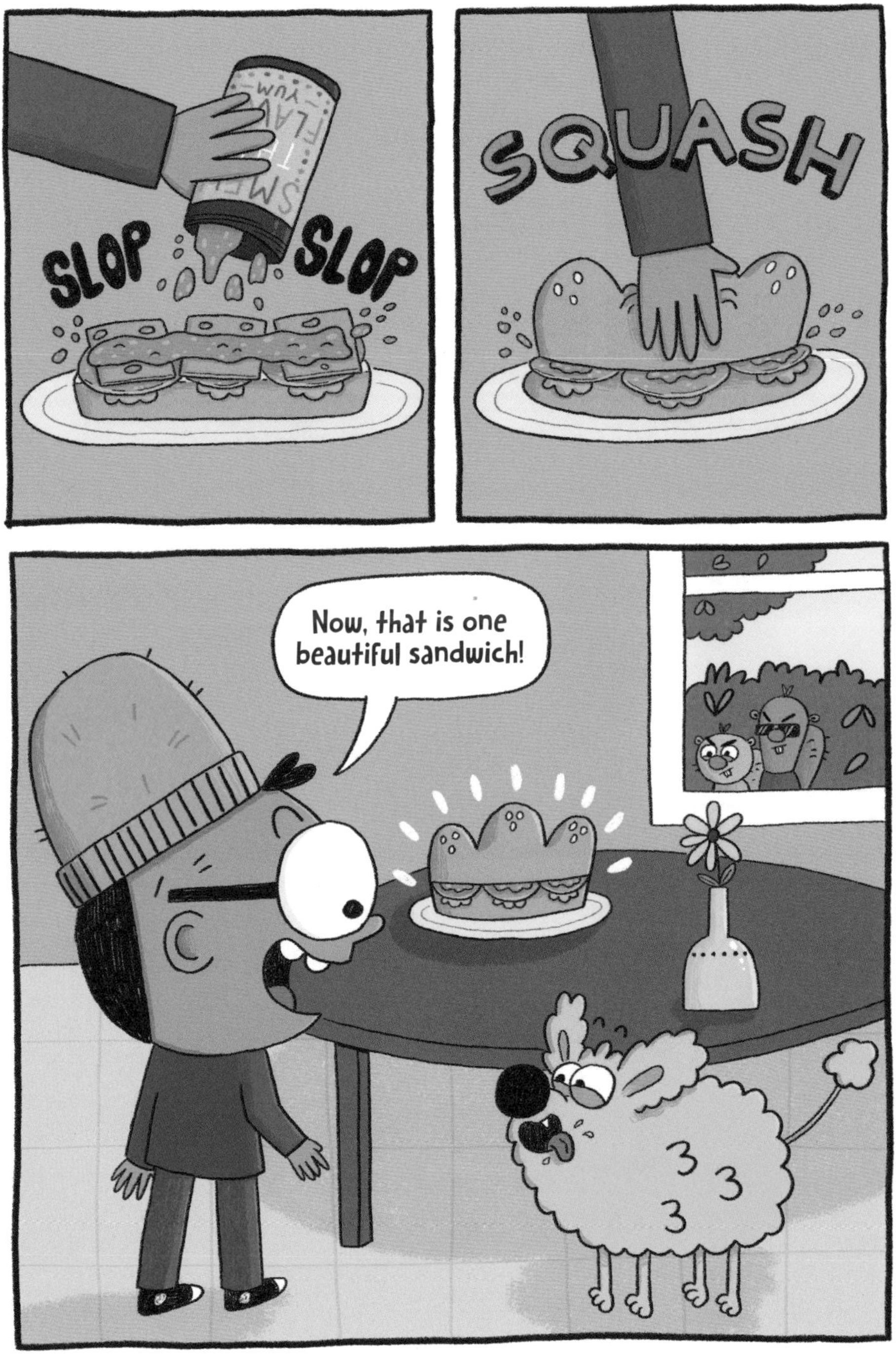
SLOP
SLOP
SQUASH
Now, that is one beautiful sandwich!

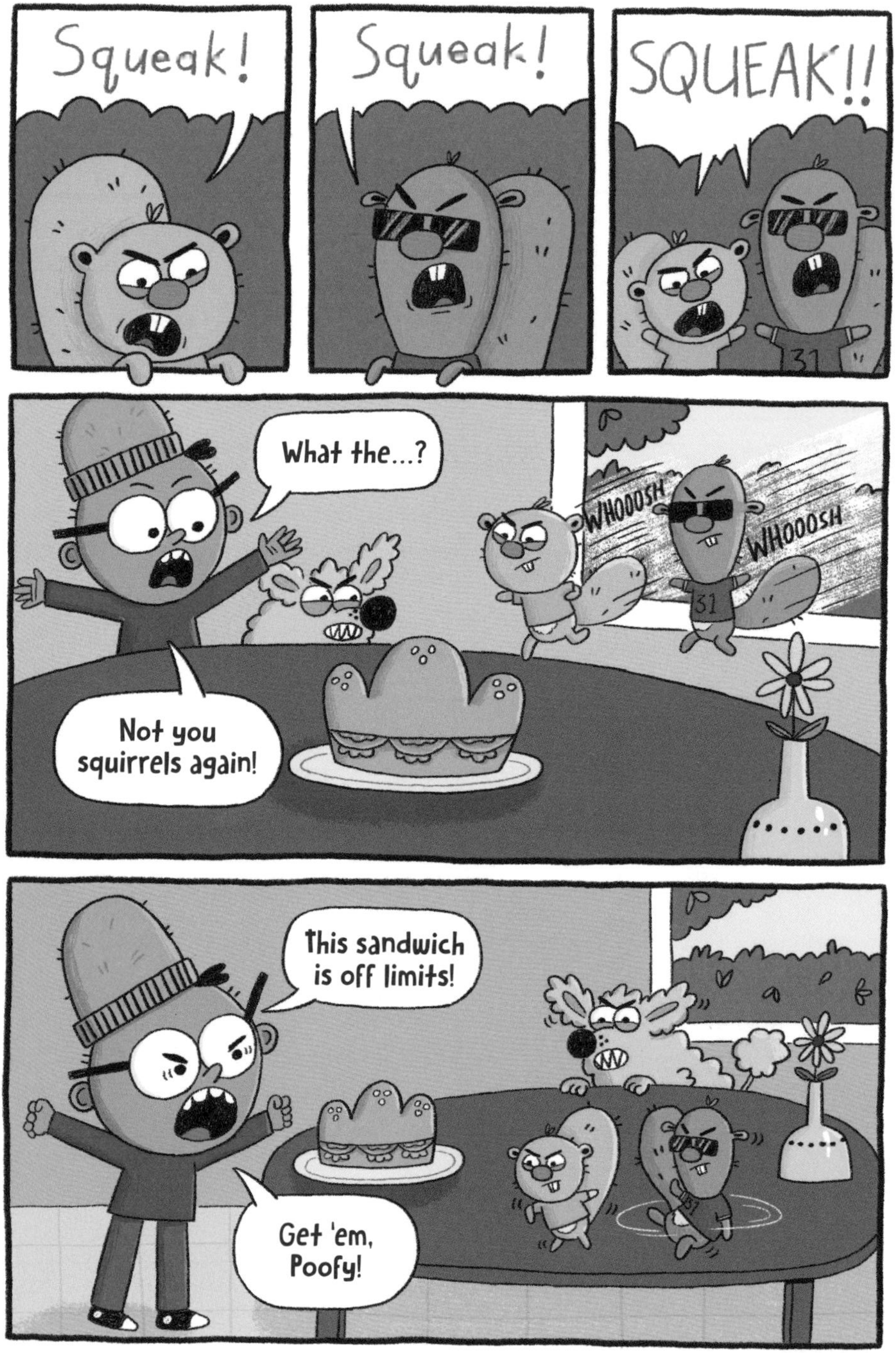
Squeak!
Squeak!
SQUEAK!!
What the...?
WHOOOSH
WHOOOSH
31
Not you squirrels again!
This sandwich is off limits!
Get 'em, Poofy!

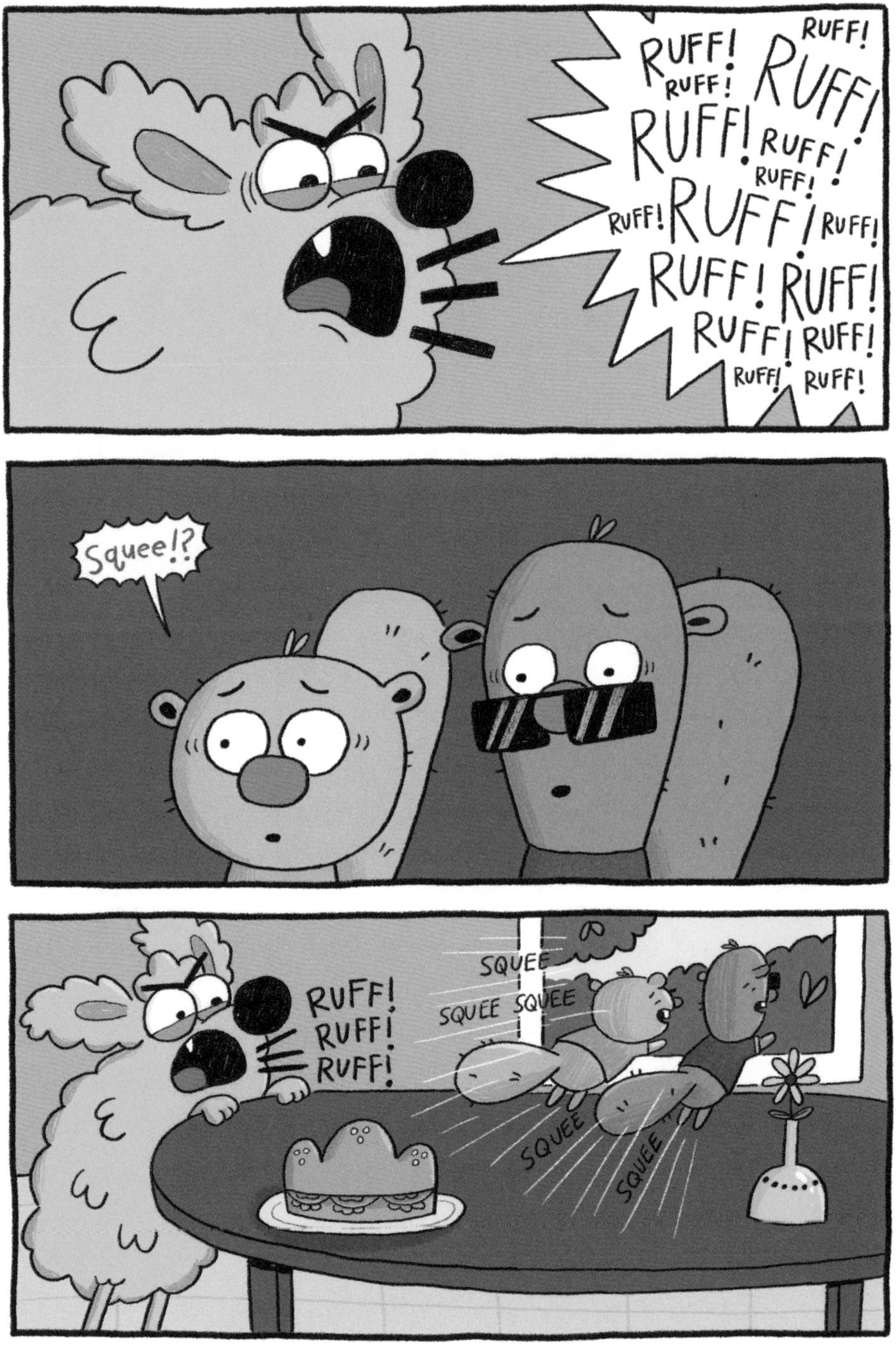

RUFF! RUFF! RUFF! RUFF! RUFF! RUFF! RUFF! RUFF! RUFF! RUFF! RUFF! RUFF! RUFF! RUFF! RUFF! RUFF! RUFF!
Squee!?
RUFF!
RUFF!
RUFF!
SQUEE
SQUEE SQUEE
SQUEE
SQUEE

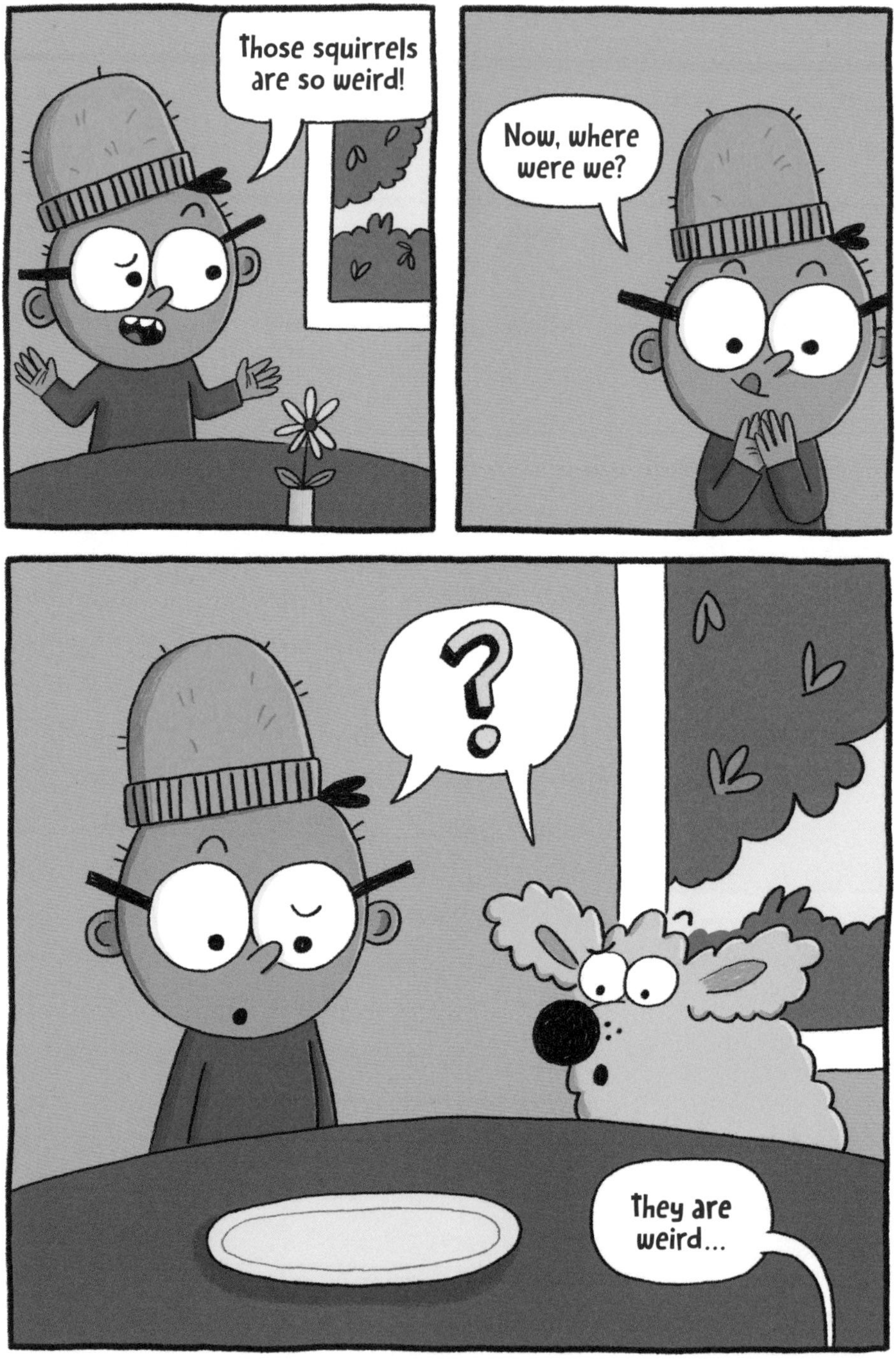
Those squirrels are so weird!
Now, where were we?
?
They are weird...

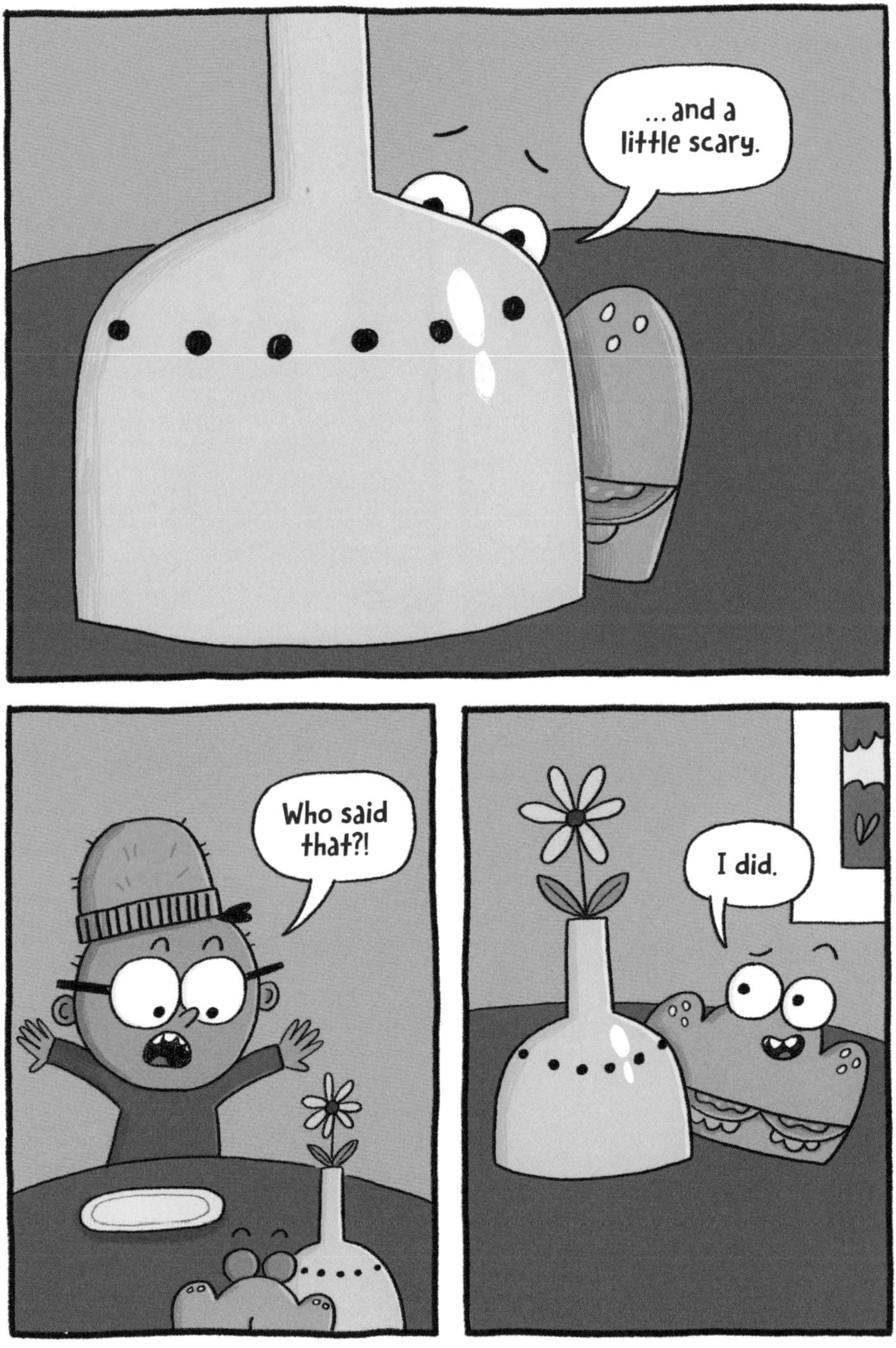
...and a little scary.
Who said that?!
I did.

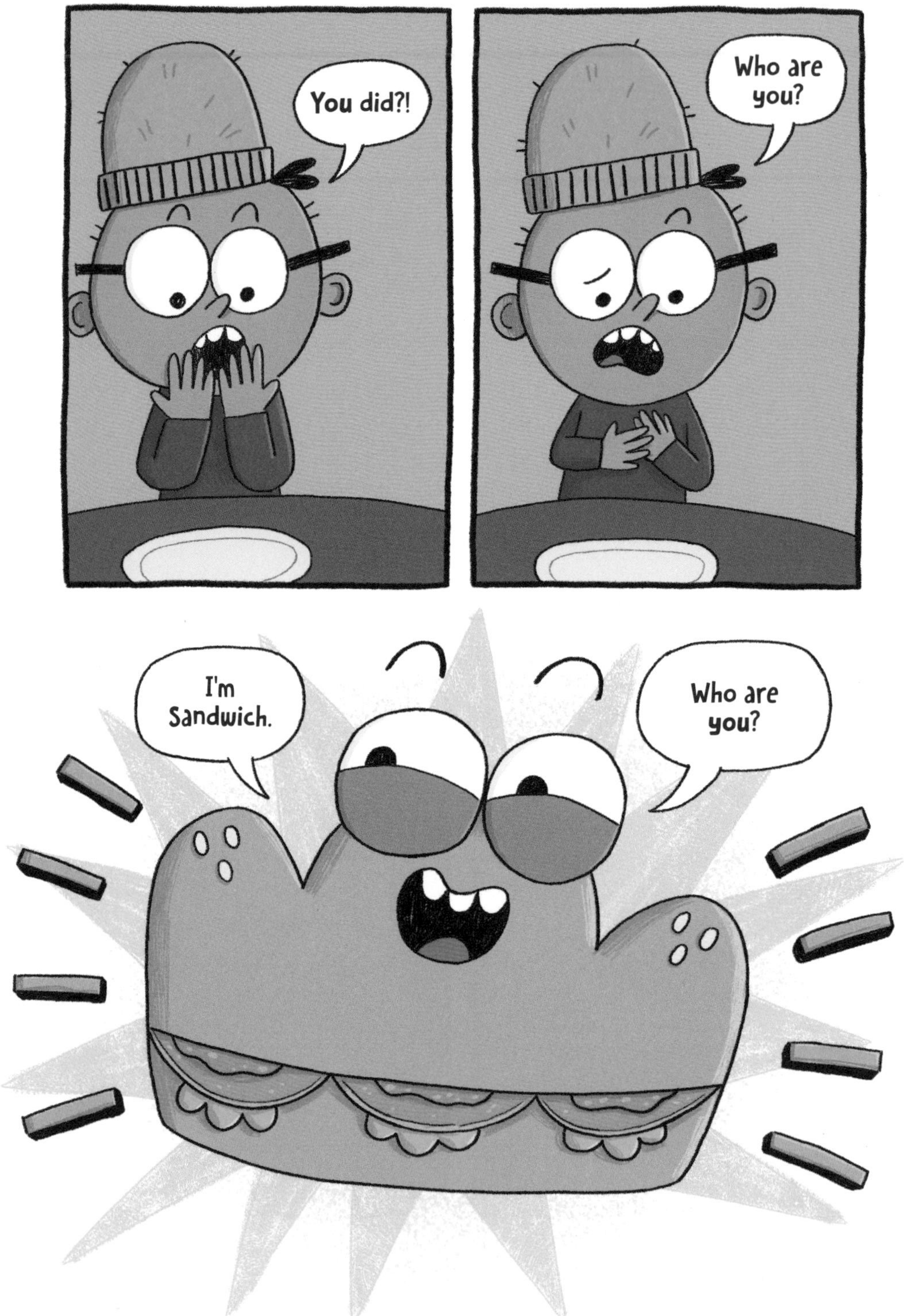
You did?!
Who are you?
I'm Sandwich.
Who are you?

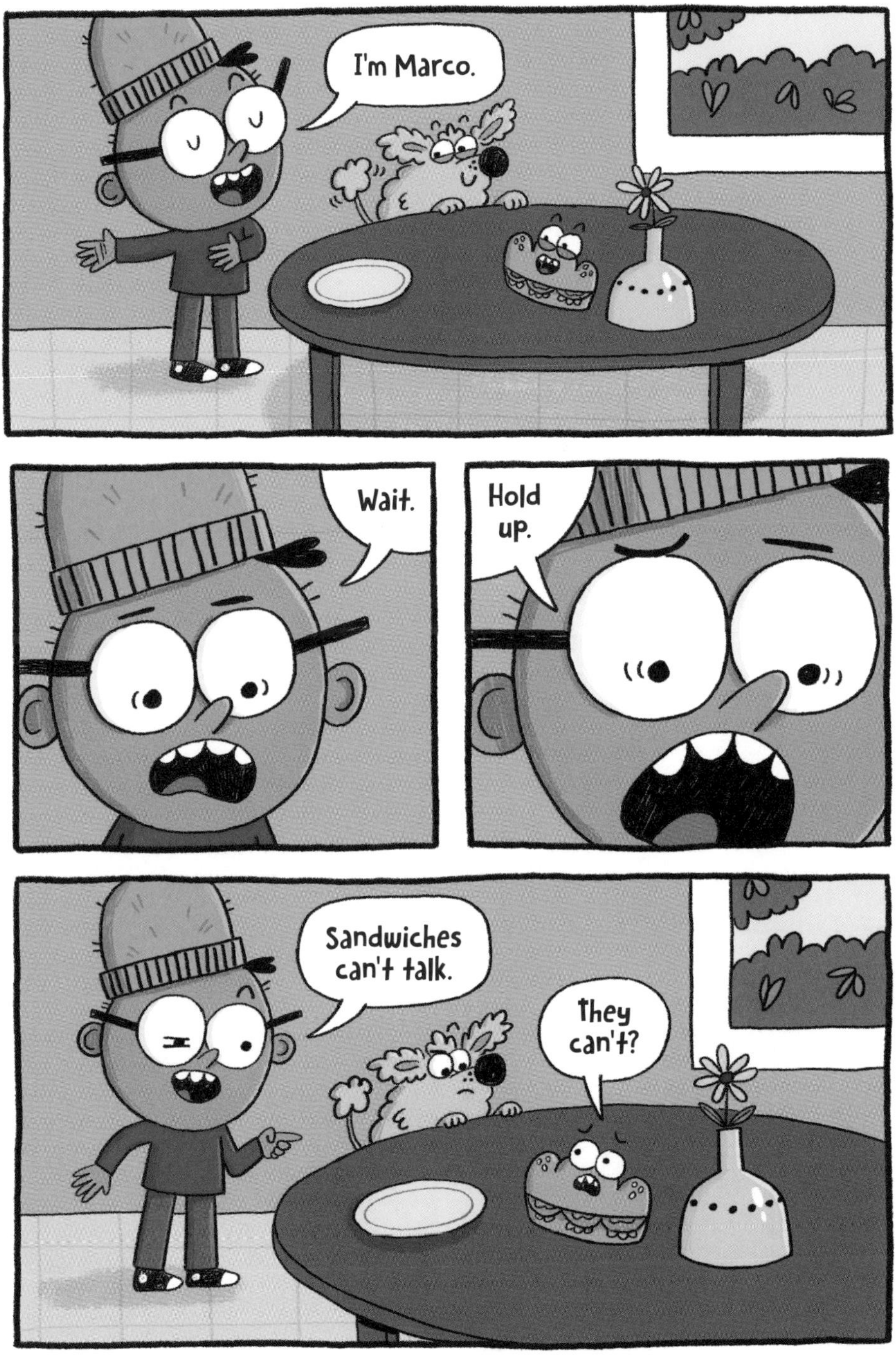
I'm Marco.
Wait.
Hold up.
Sandwiches can't talk.
they can't?

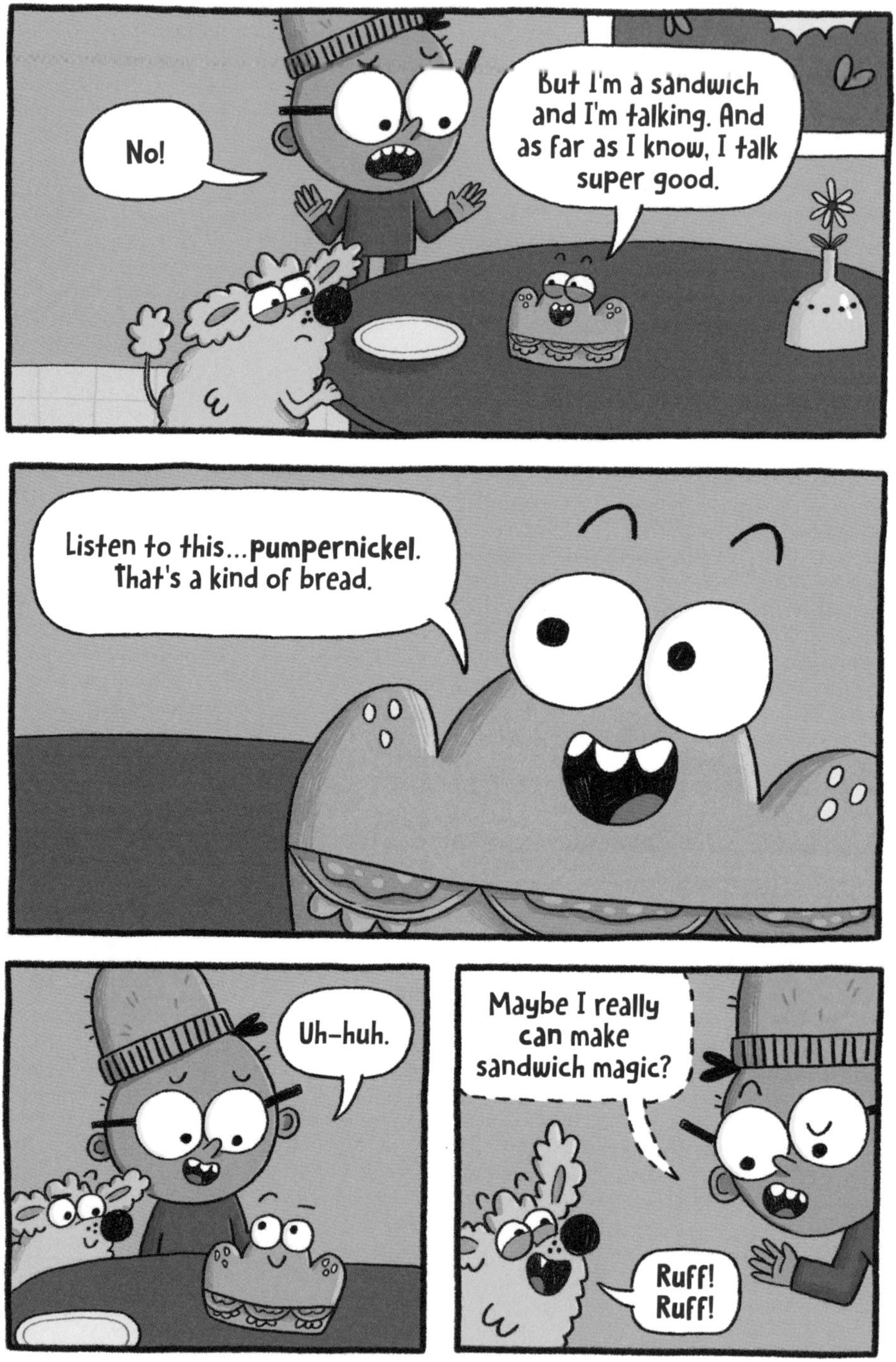
No!
But I'm a sandwich and I'm talking. And as far as I know, I talk super good.
Listen to this...pumpernickel. That's a kind of bread.
Uh-huh.
Maybe I really can make sandwich magic?
Ruff! Ruff!

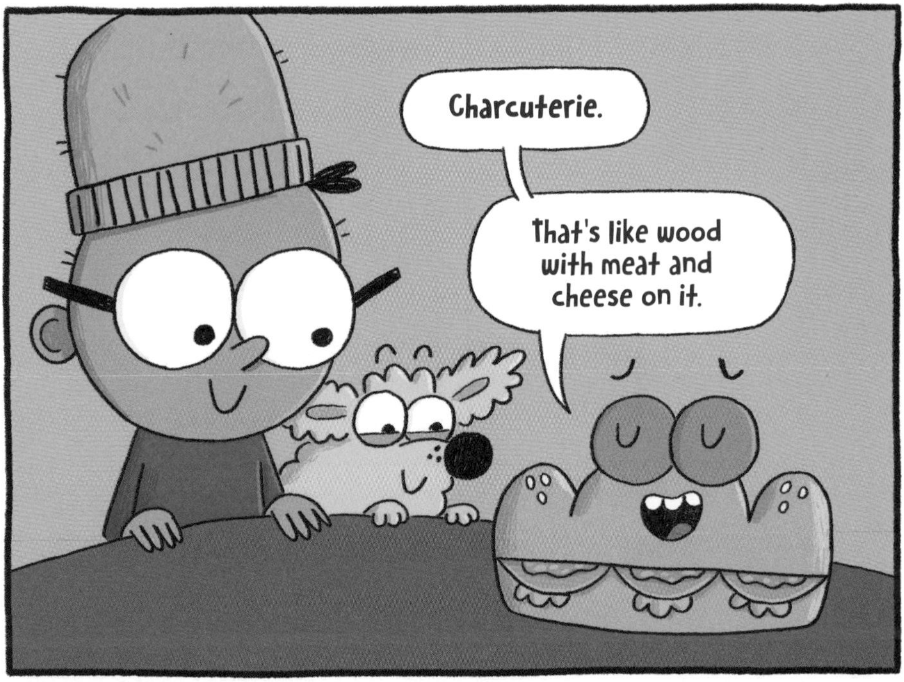
Charcuterie.
That's like wood with meat and cheese on it.

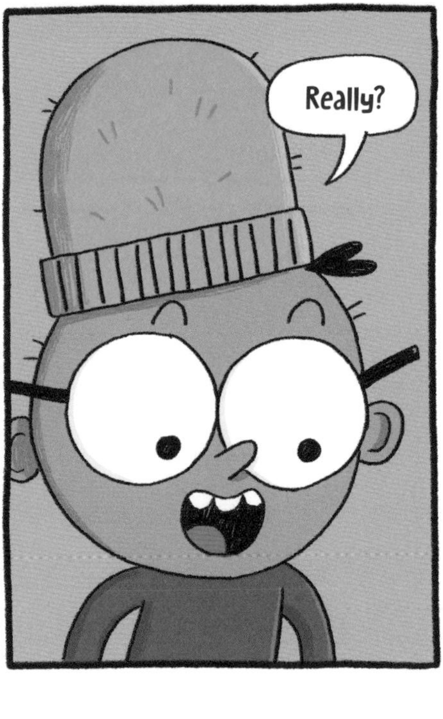
Really?

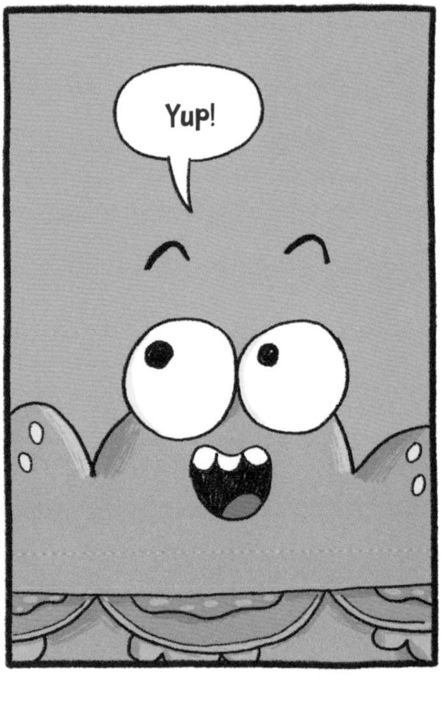
Yup!

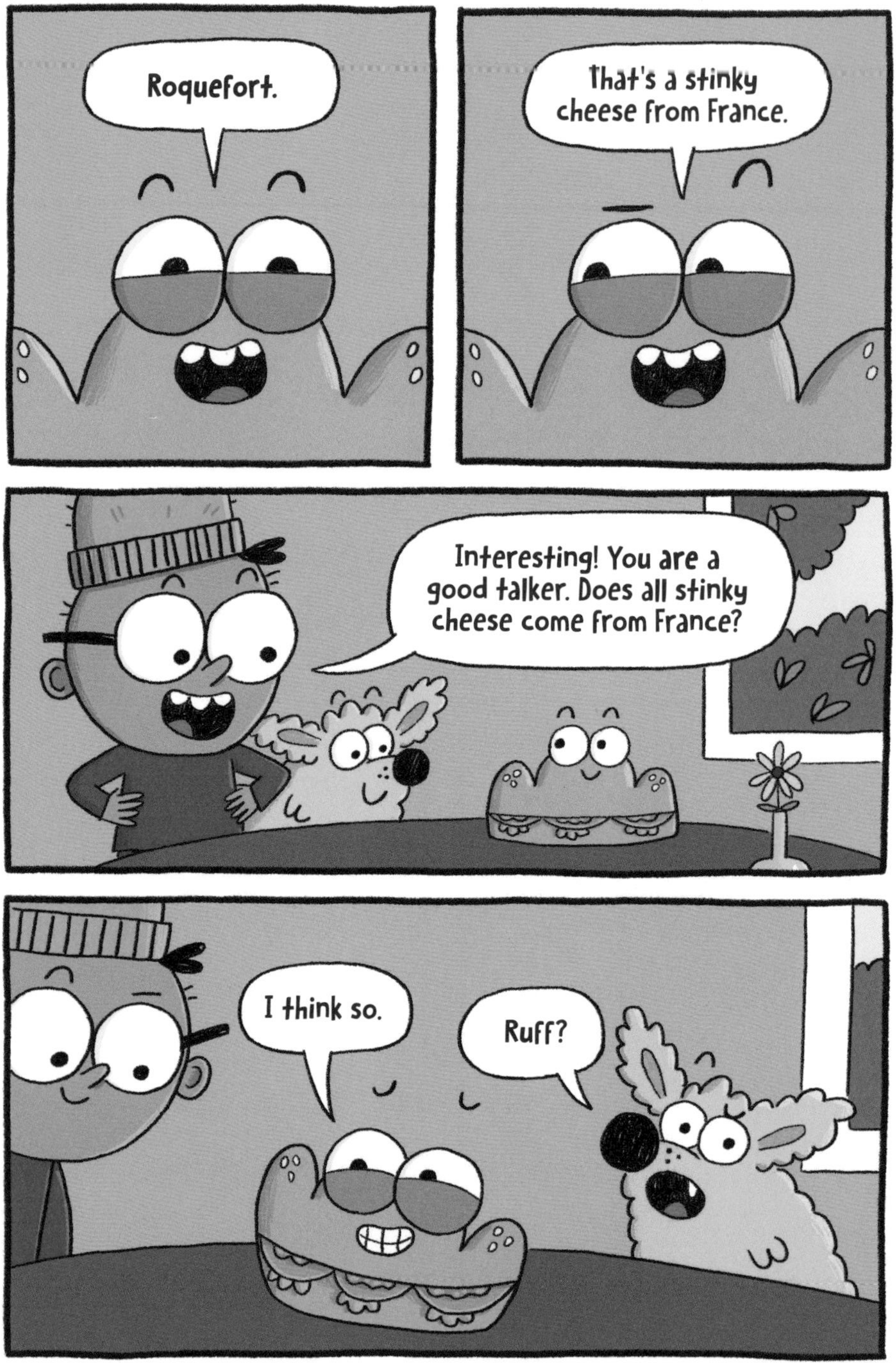
Roquefort.
That's a stinky cheese from France.
Interesting! You are a good talker. Does all stinky cheese come from France?
I think so.
Ruff?

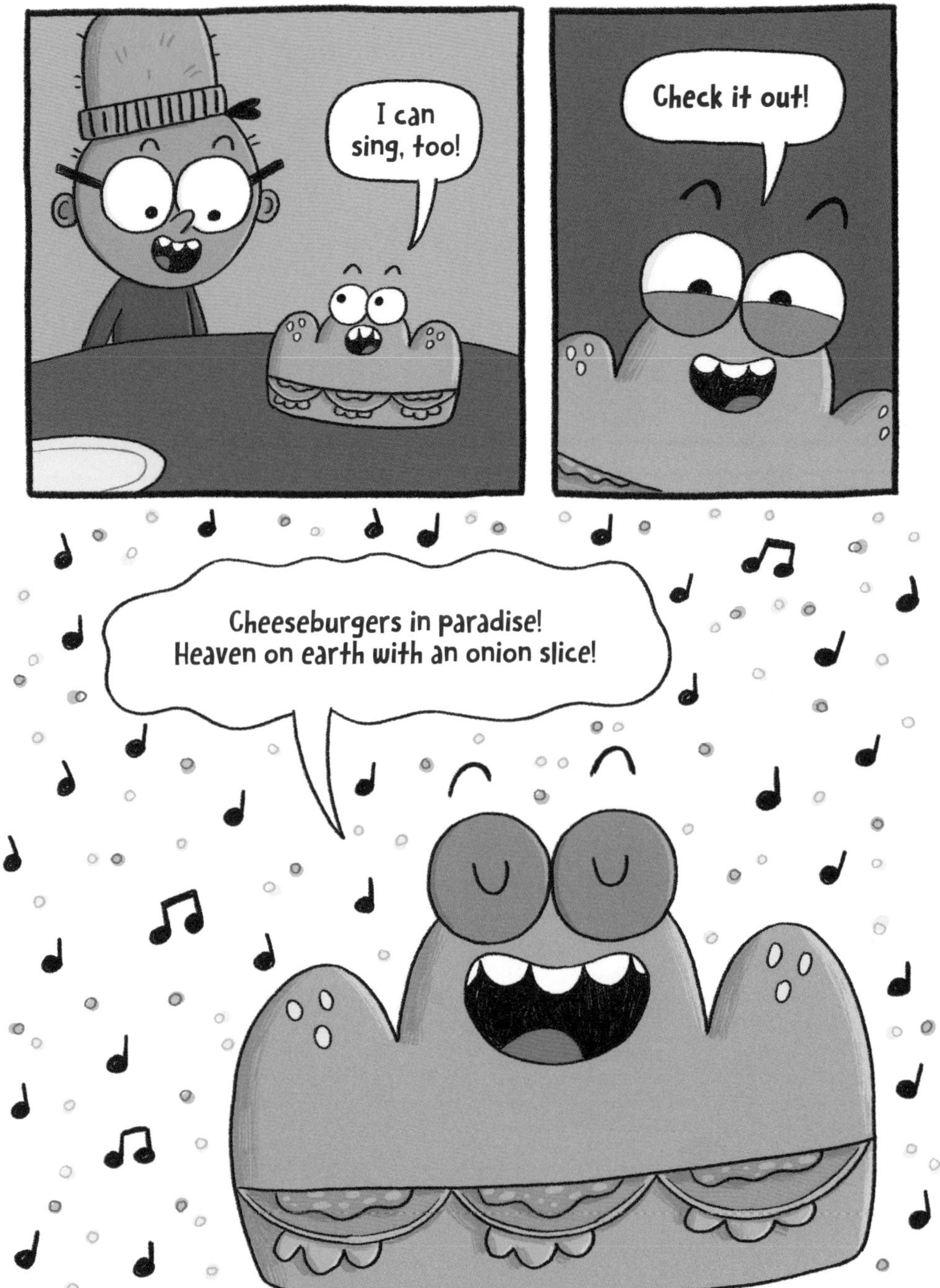
I can sing, too!
Check it out!
Cheeseburgers in paradise!
Heaven on earth with an onion slice!

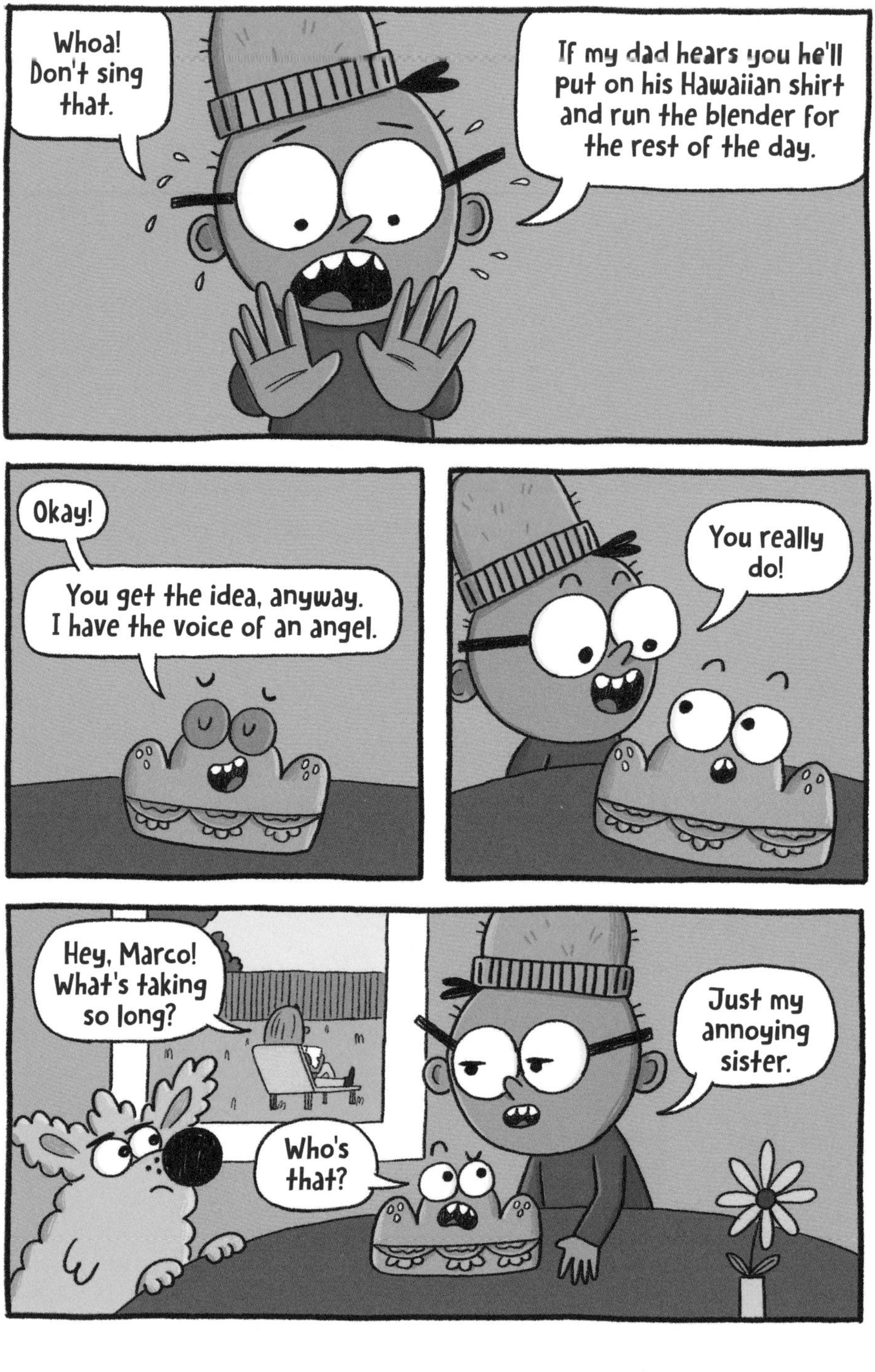
Whoa! Don't sing that.
If my dad hears you he'll put on his Hawaiian shirt and run the blender for the rest of the day.
Okay!
You get the idea, anyway. I have the voice of an angel.
You really do!
Hey, Marco! What's taking so long?
Who's that?
Just my annoying sister.

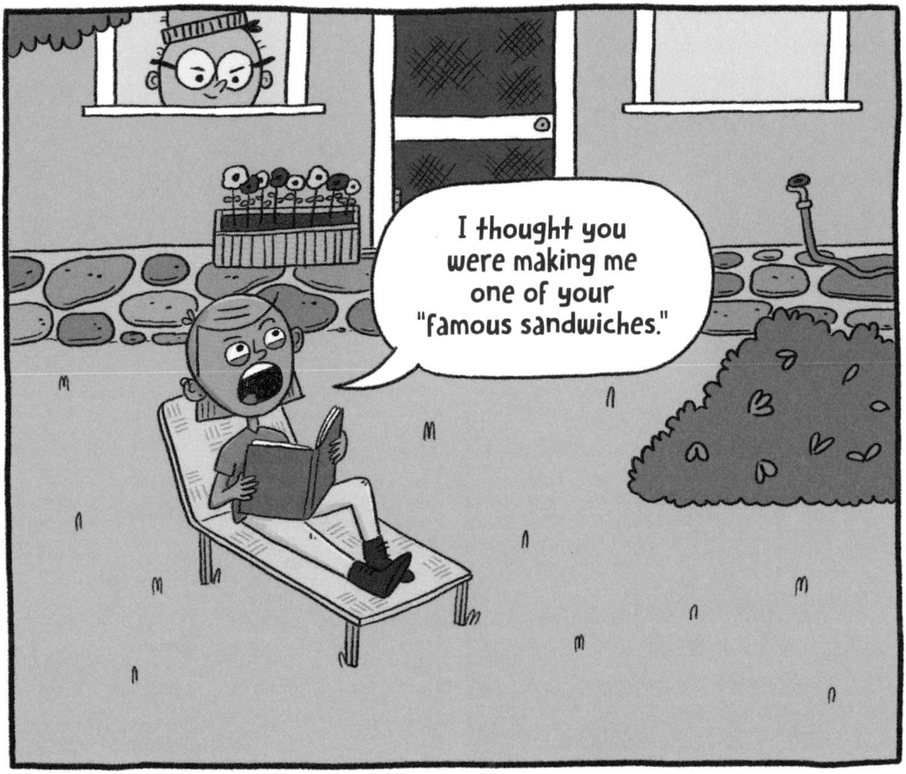
I thought you were making me one of your "famous sandwiches."

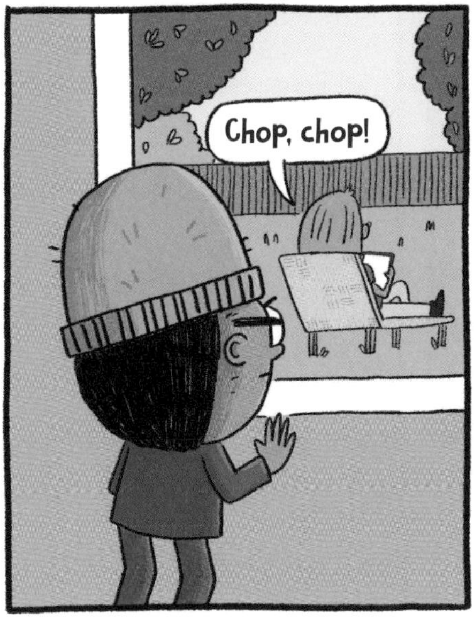
Chop, chop!

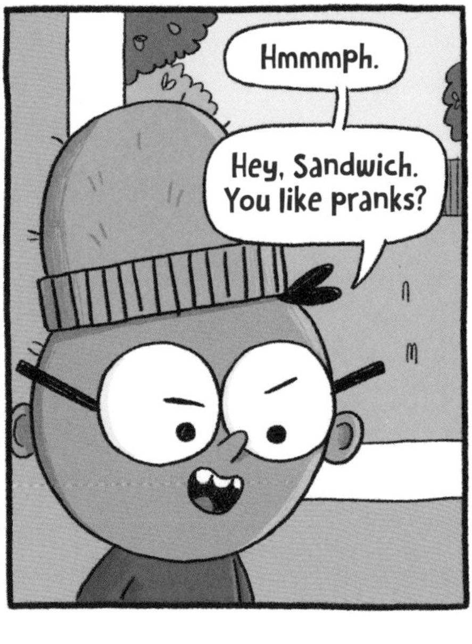
Hmmmph.
Hey, Sandwich. You like pranks?

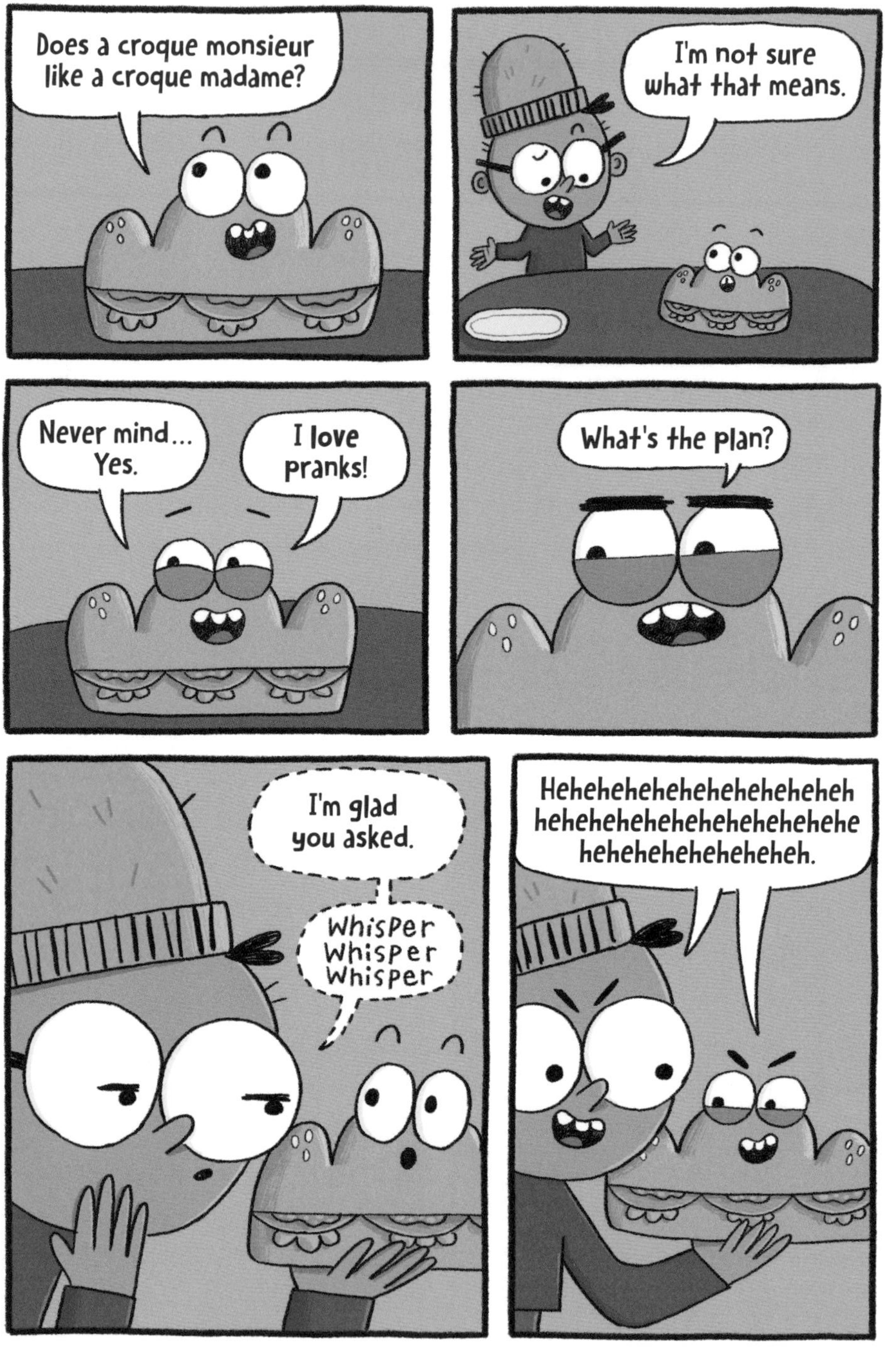
Does a croque monsieur like a croque madame?
I'm not sure what that means.
Never mind... Yes.
I love pranks!
What's the plan?
I'm glad you asked.
Whisper Whisper Whisper
Hehehehehehehehehehehehh hehehehehehehehehehehehe hehehehehehehehehh.

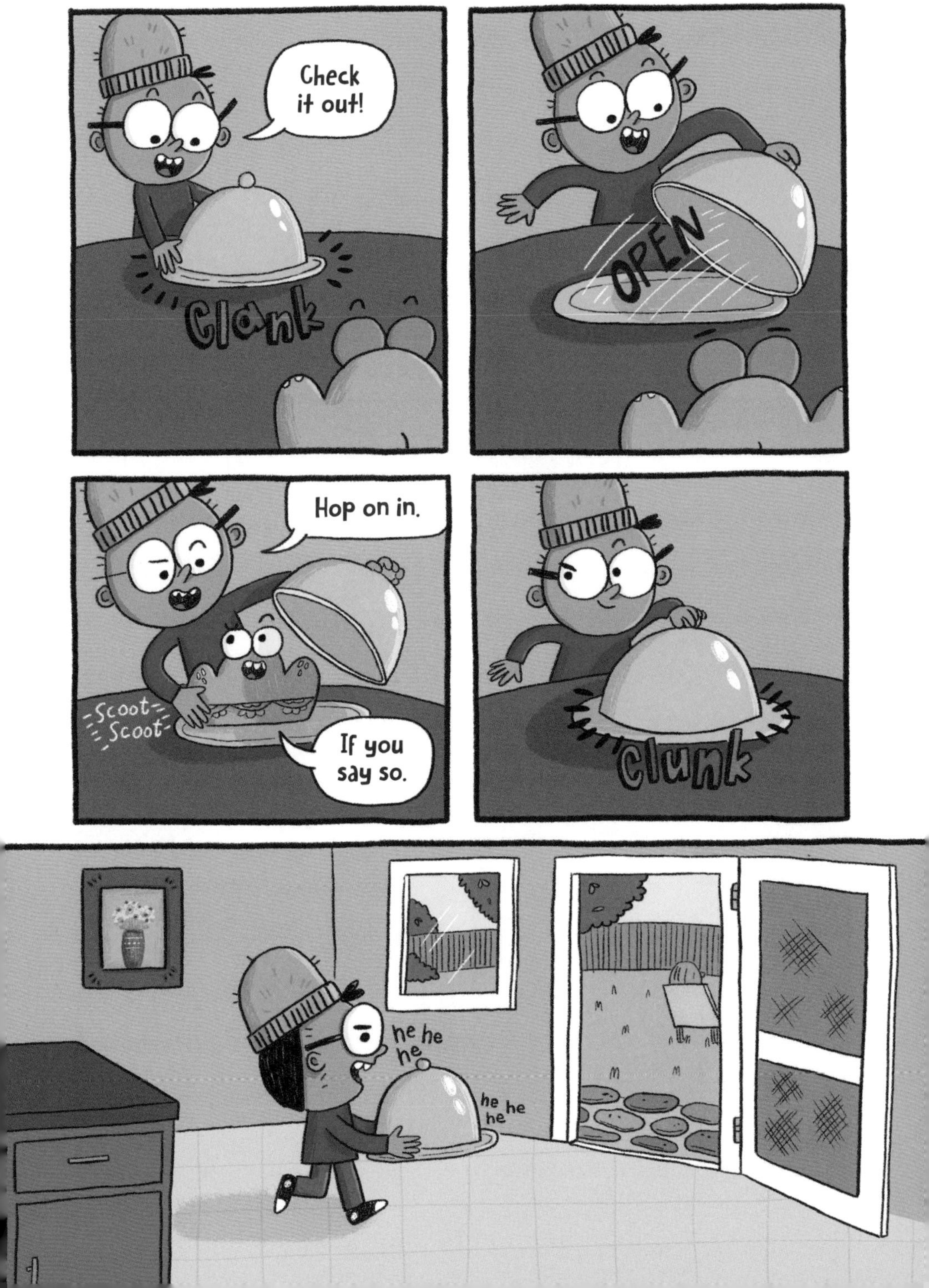
Check it out!
Clank
OPEN
Hop on in.
Scoot Scoot
If you say so.
Clunk
he he he
he he he

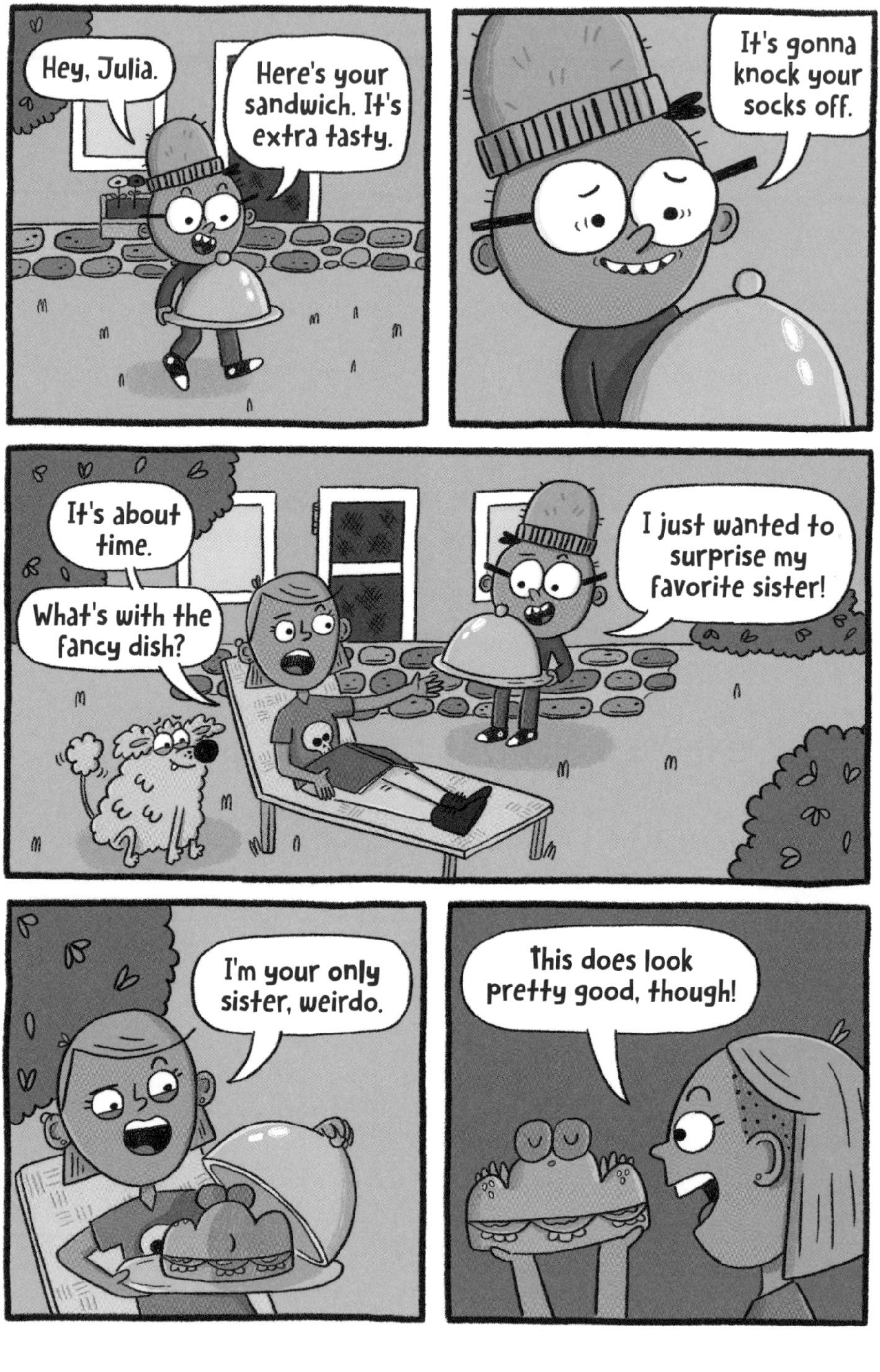
Hey, Julia.
Here's your sandwich. It's extra tasty.
It's gonna knock your socks off.
It's about time.
What's with the fancy dish?
I just wanted to surprise my favorite sister!
I'm your only sister, weirdo.
This does look pretty good, though!

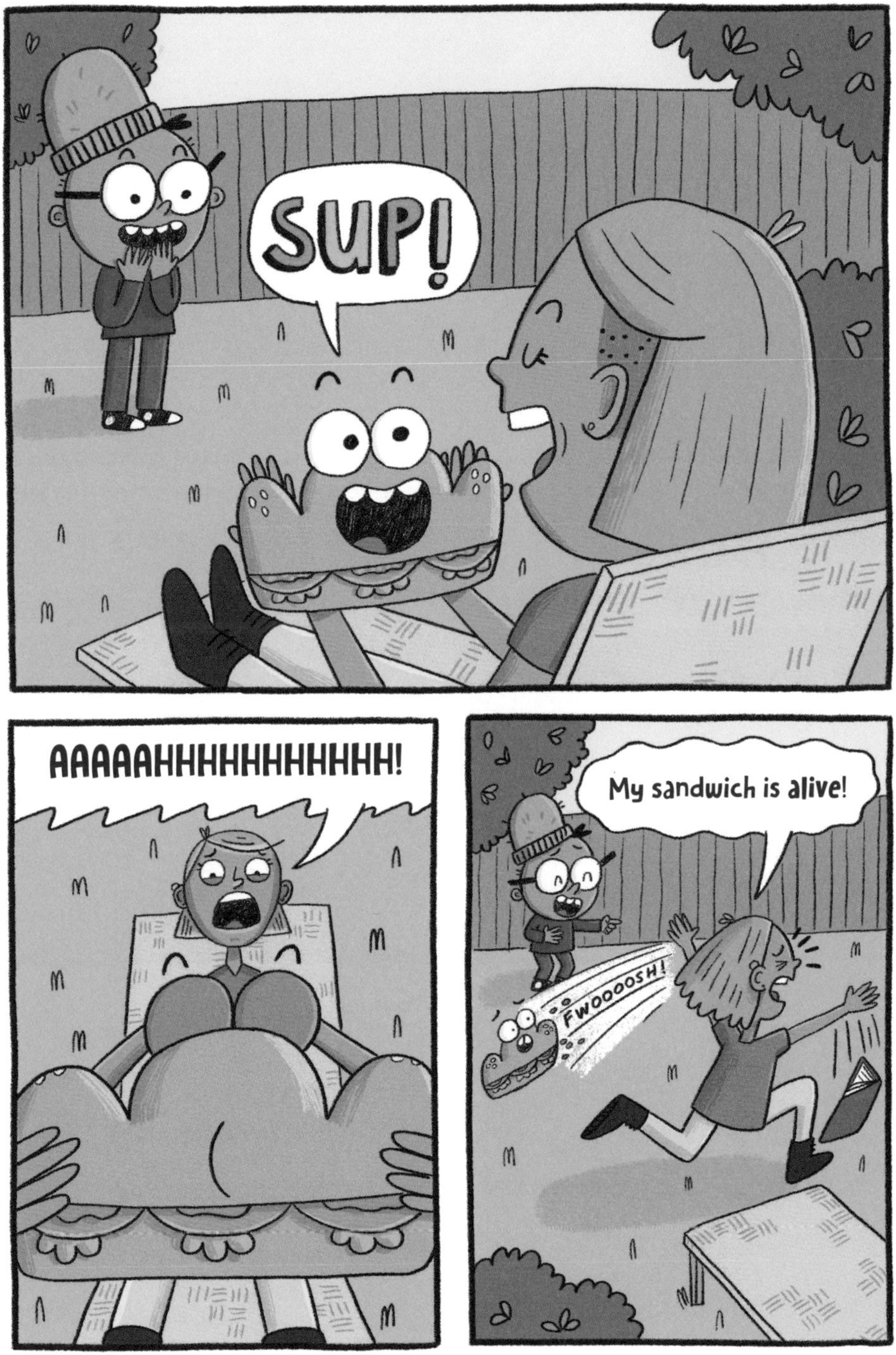
SUP!
AAAAAHHHHHHHHHHH!
My sandwich is alive!
FWOOOOSH!

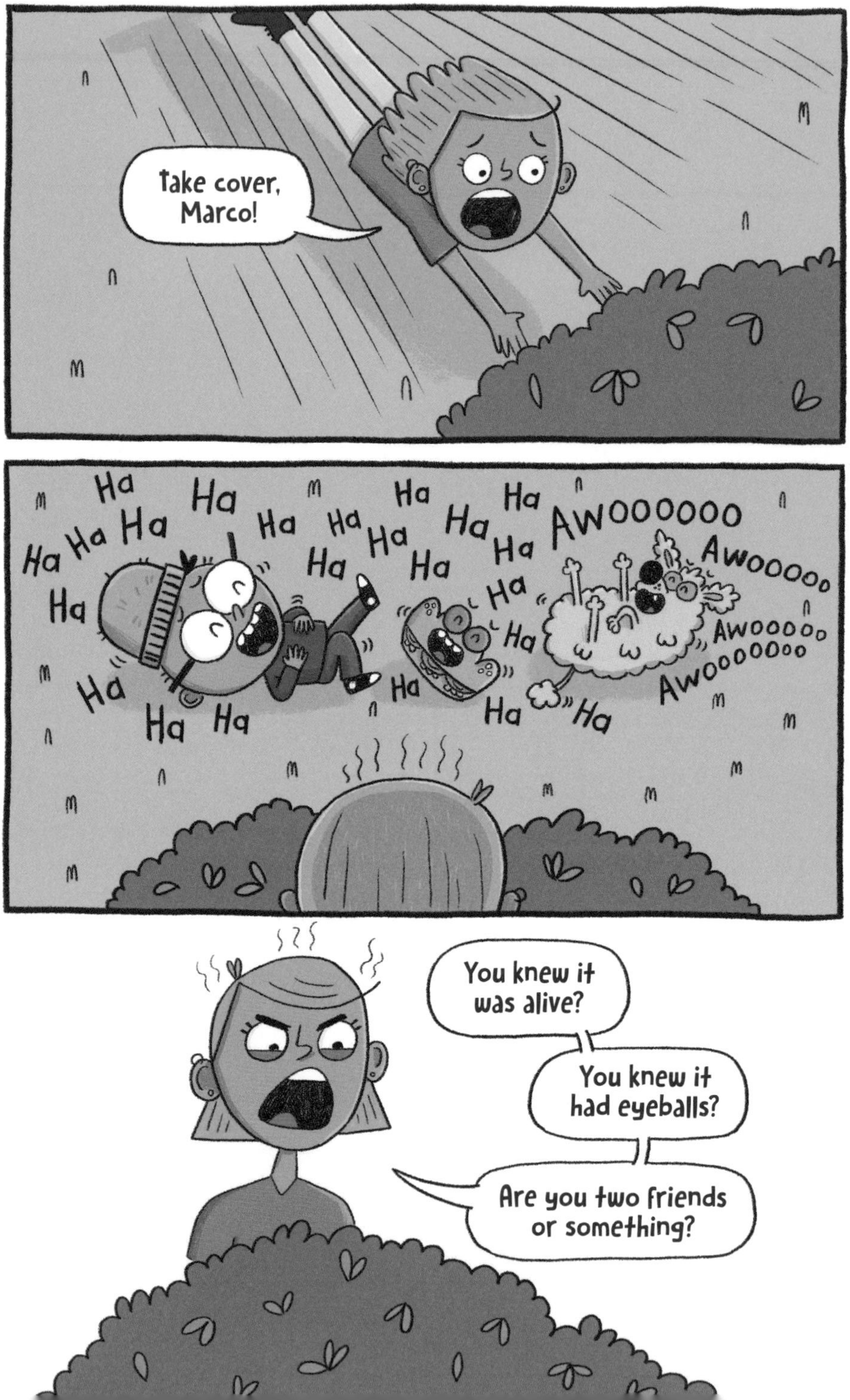
take cover, Marco!
Ha Ha Ha Ha Ha Ha Ha Ha Ha Ha Ha Ha Ha Ha Ha Ha Ha Ha Ha Ha Ha
Awooooooo
Awoooooo
Awoooooo
Awooooooooo
You knew it was alive?
You knew it had eyeballs?
Are you two friends or something?

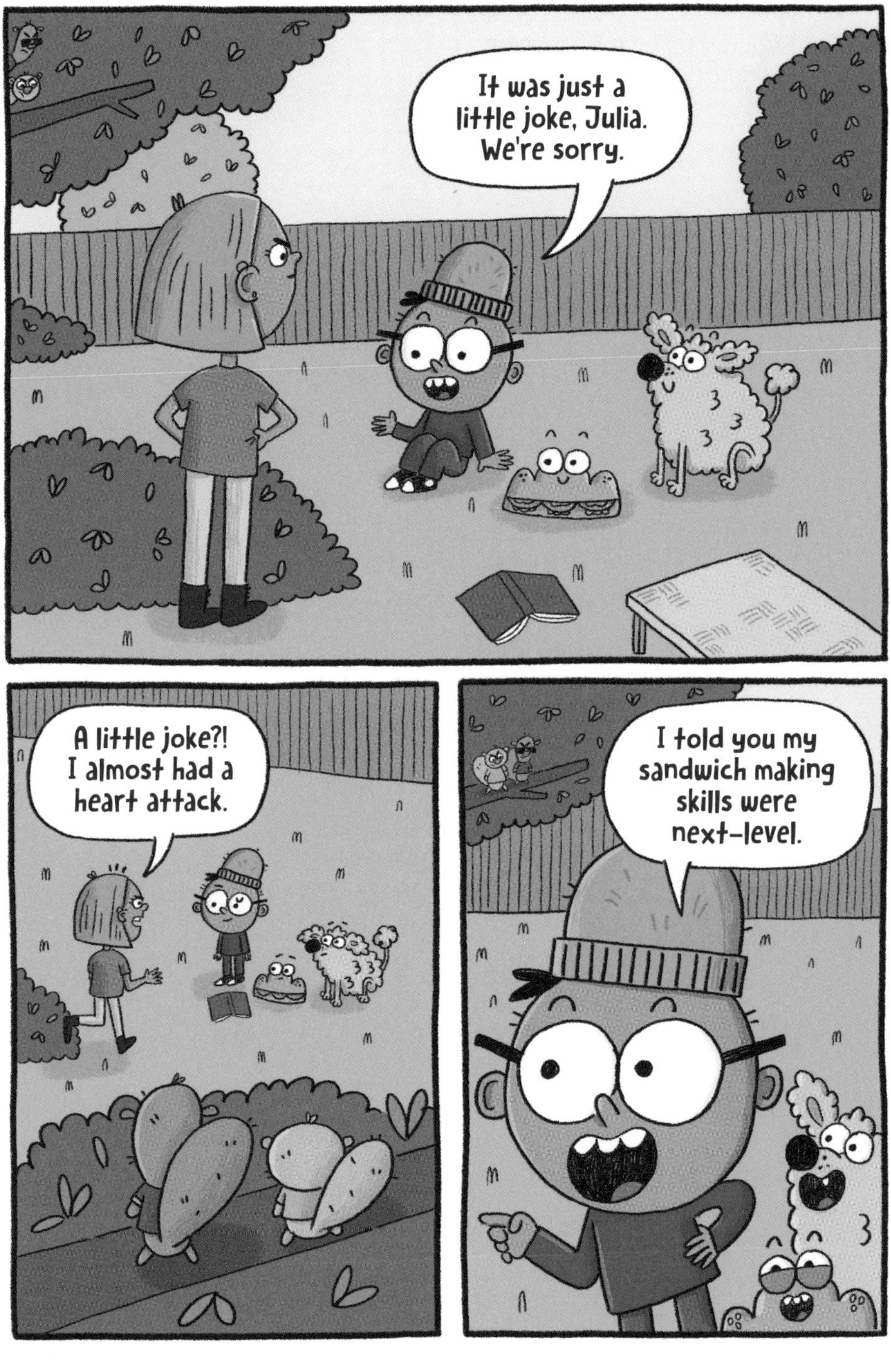
It was just a little joke, Julia. We're sorry.
A little joke?! I almost had a heart attack.
I told you my sandwich making skills were next-level.

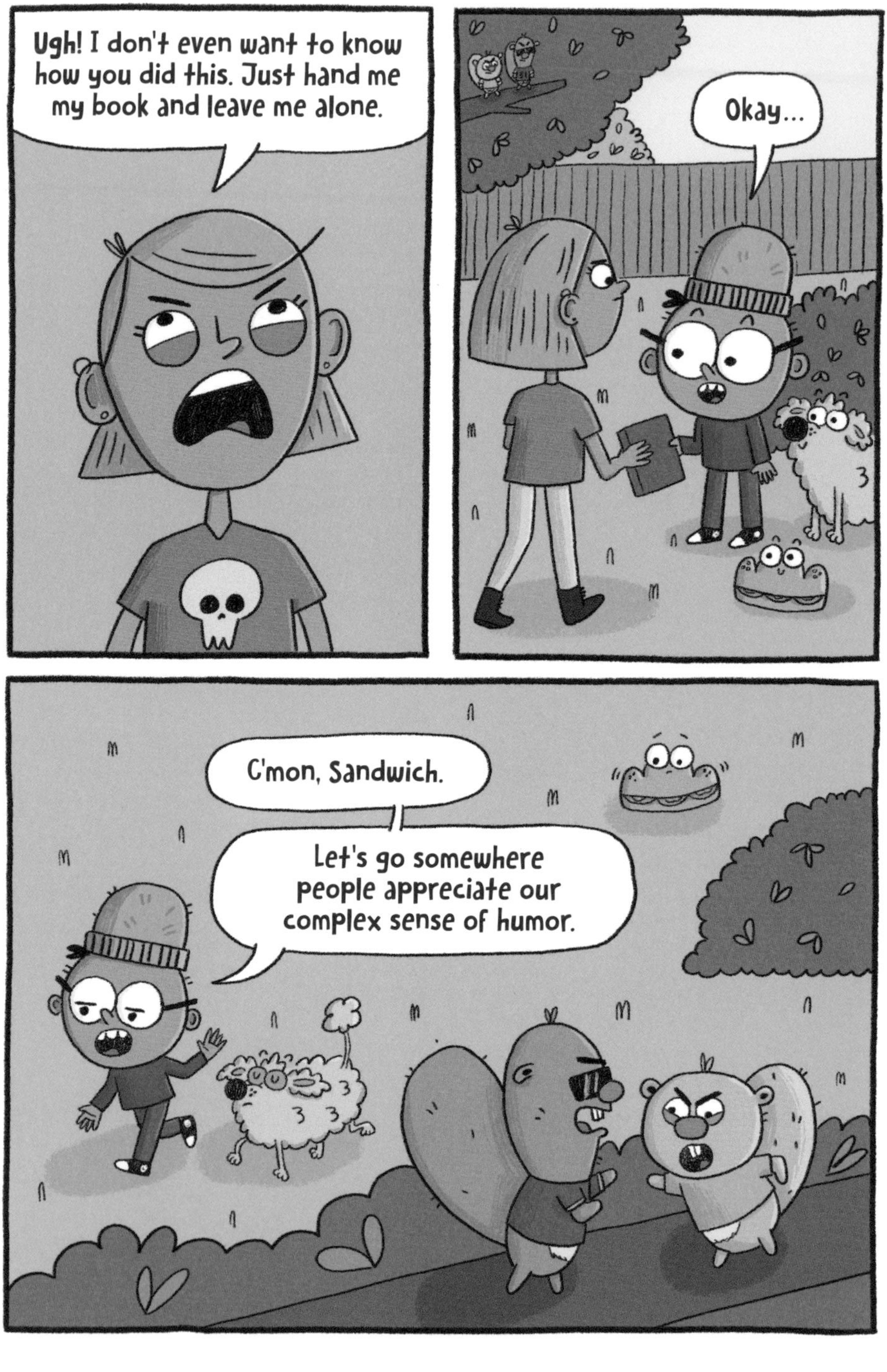
Ugh! I don't even want to know how you did this. Just hand me my book and leave me alone.
Okay...
C'mon, Sandwich.
Let's go somewhere people appreciate our complex sense of humor.

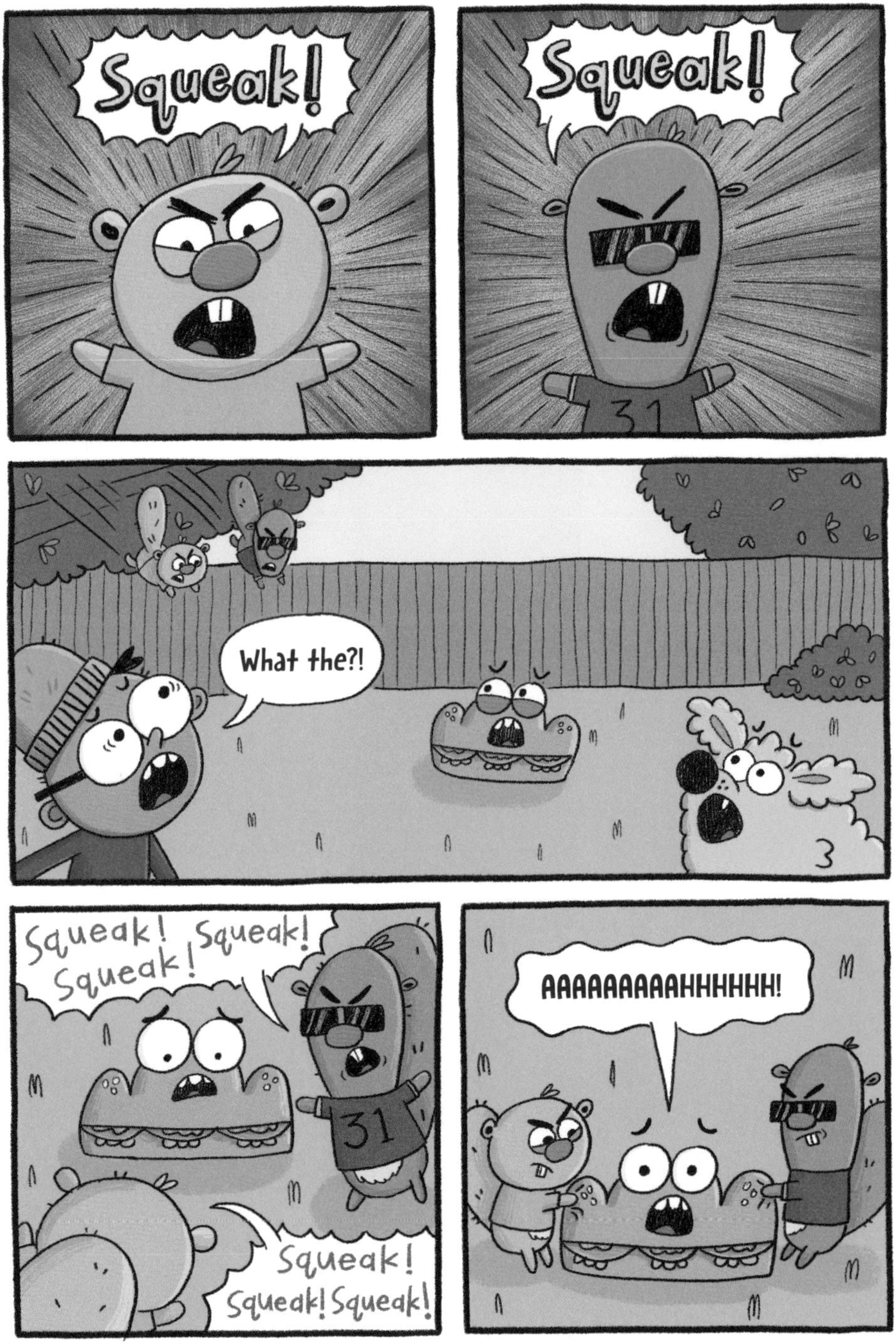
Squeak!
Squeak!
What the?!
Squeak! Squeak! Squeak!
Squeak! Squeak! Squeak!
AAAAAAAAAHHHHHH!

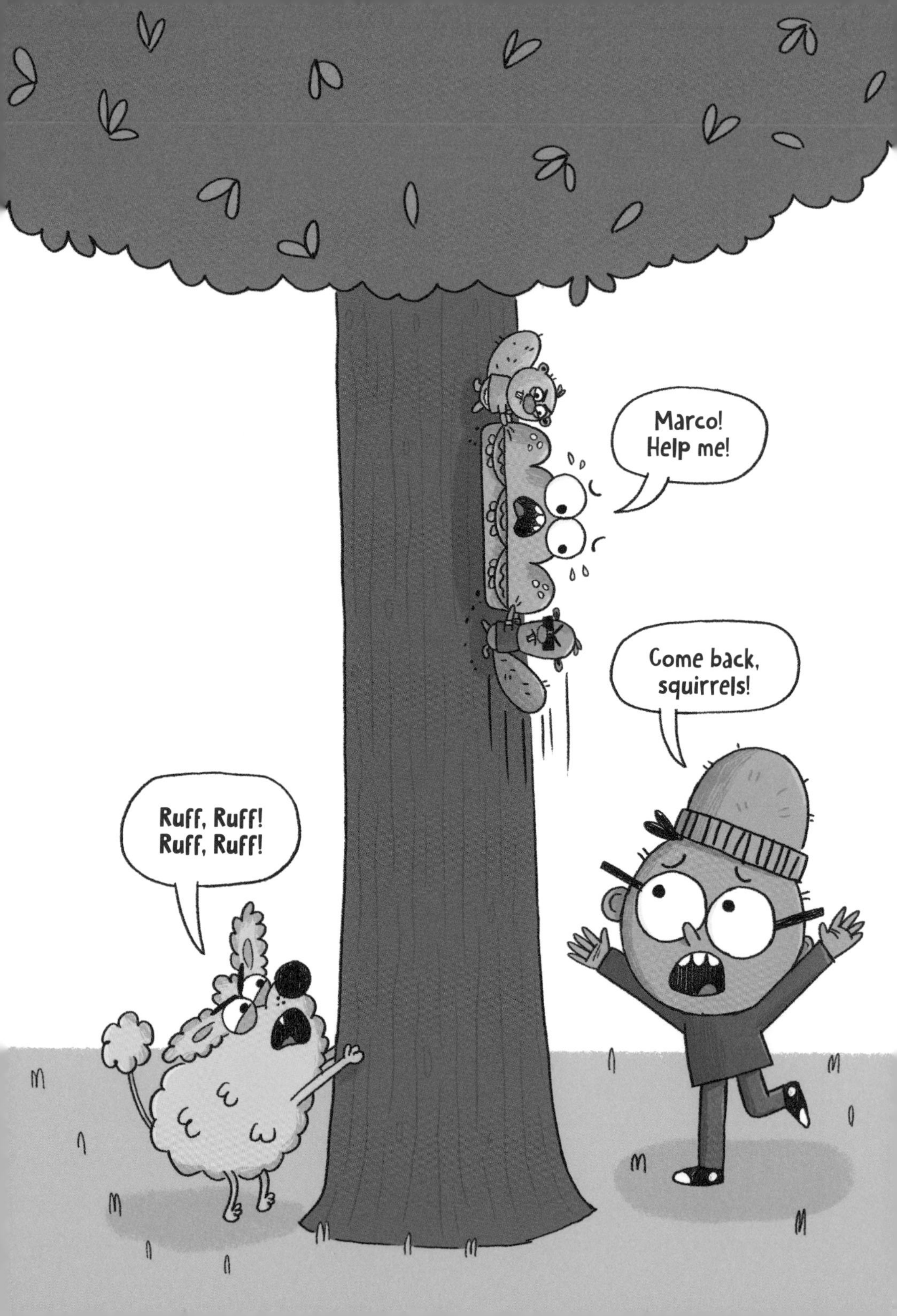
Marco!
Help me!
Come back,
squirrels!
Ruff, Ruff!
Ruff, Ruff!

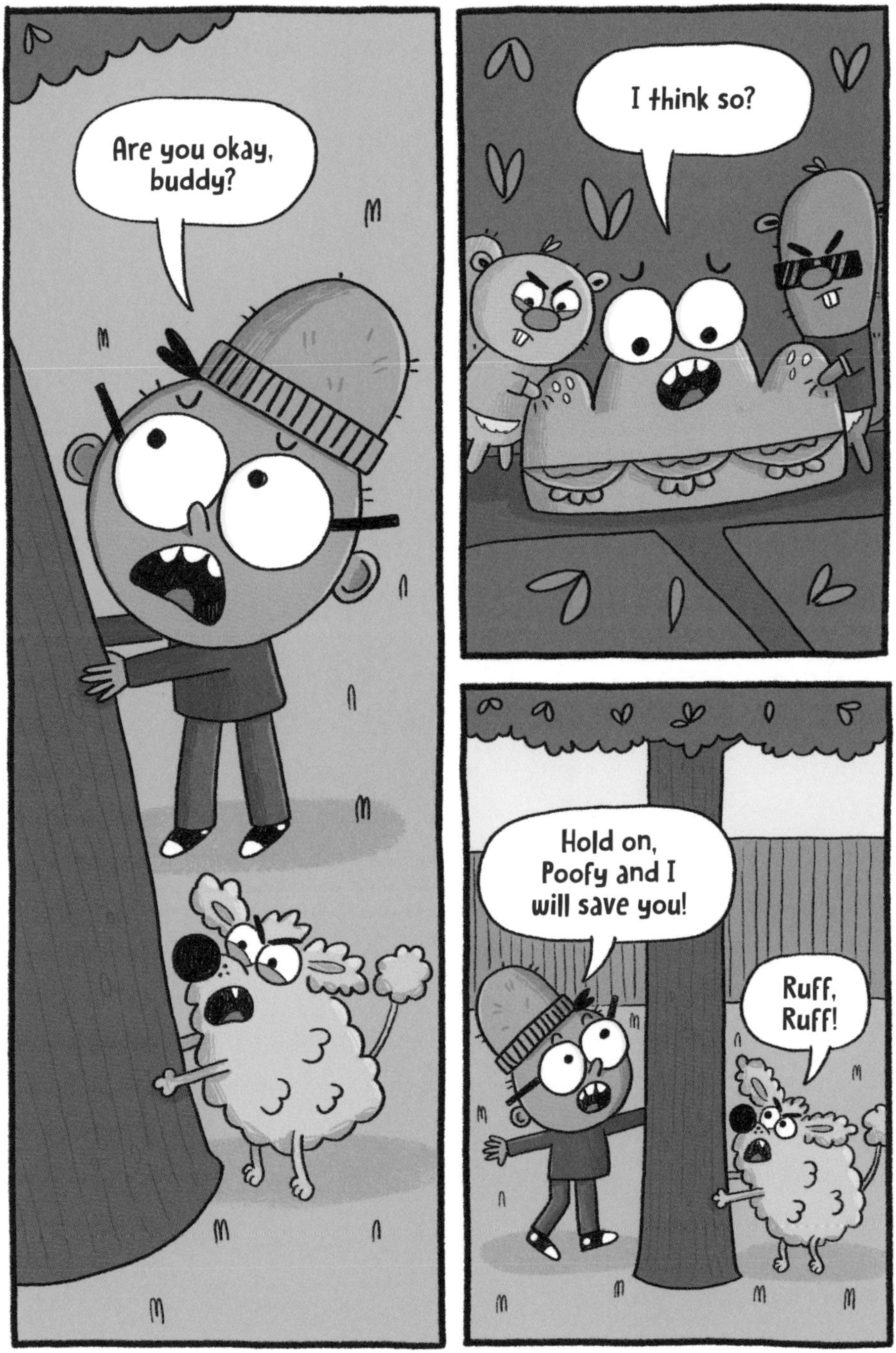
Are you okay, buddy?
I think so?
Hold on, Poofy and I will save you!
Ruff, Ruff!

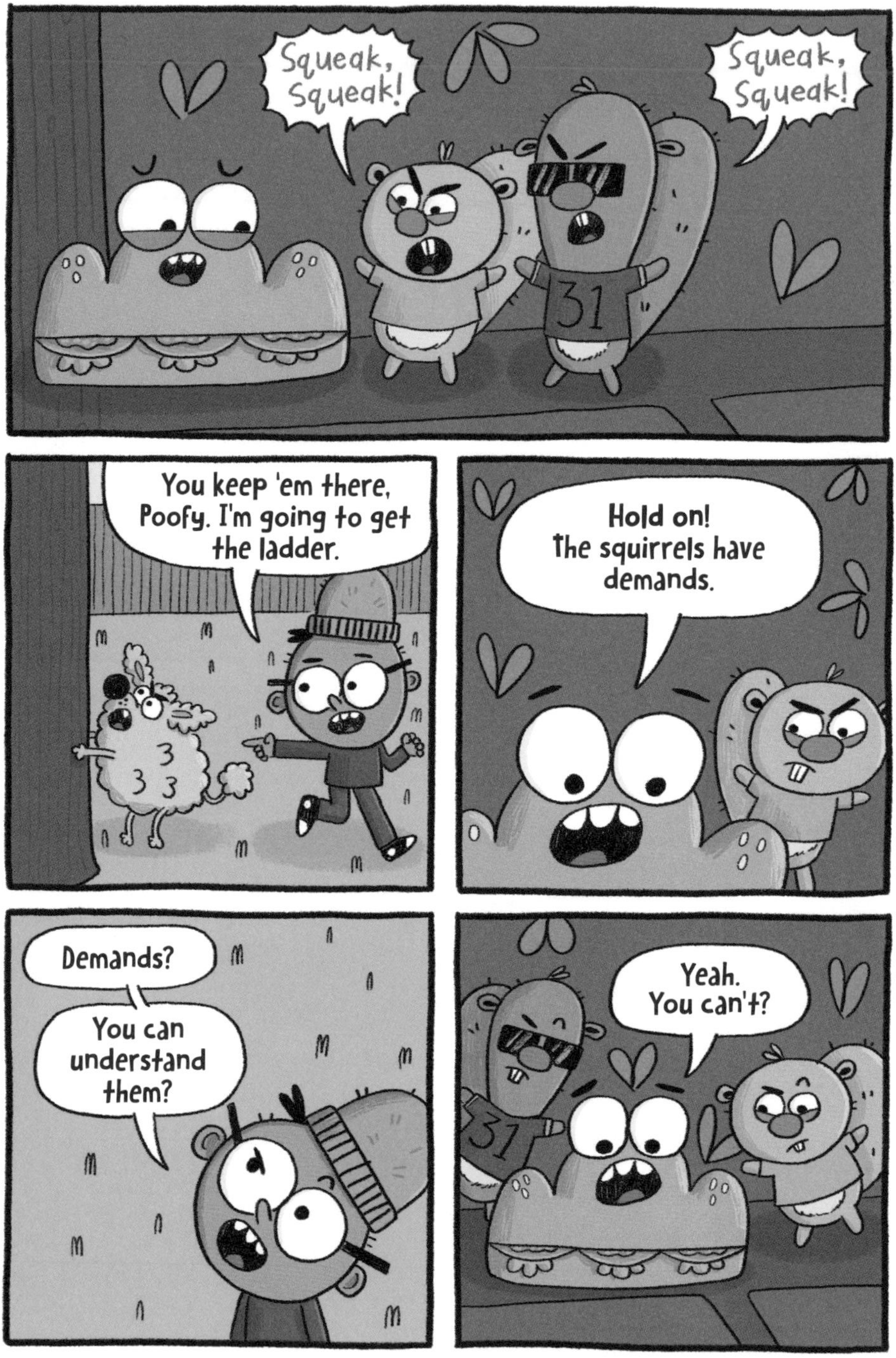
Squeak, Squeak!
Squeak, Squeak!
31
You keep 'em there, Poofy. I'm going to get the ladder.
Hold on! The squirrels have demands.
Demands?
You can understand them?
Yeah. You can't?
31

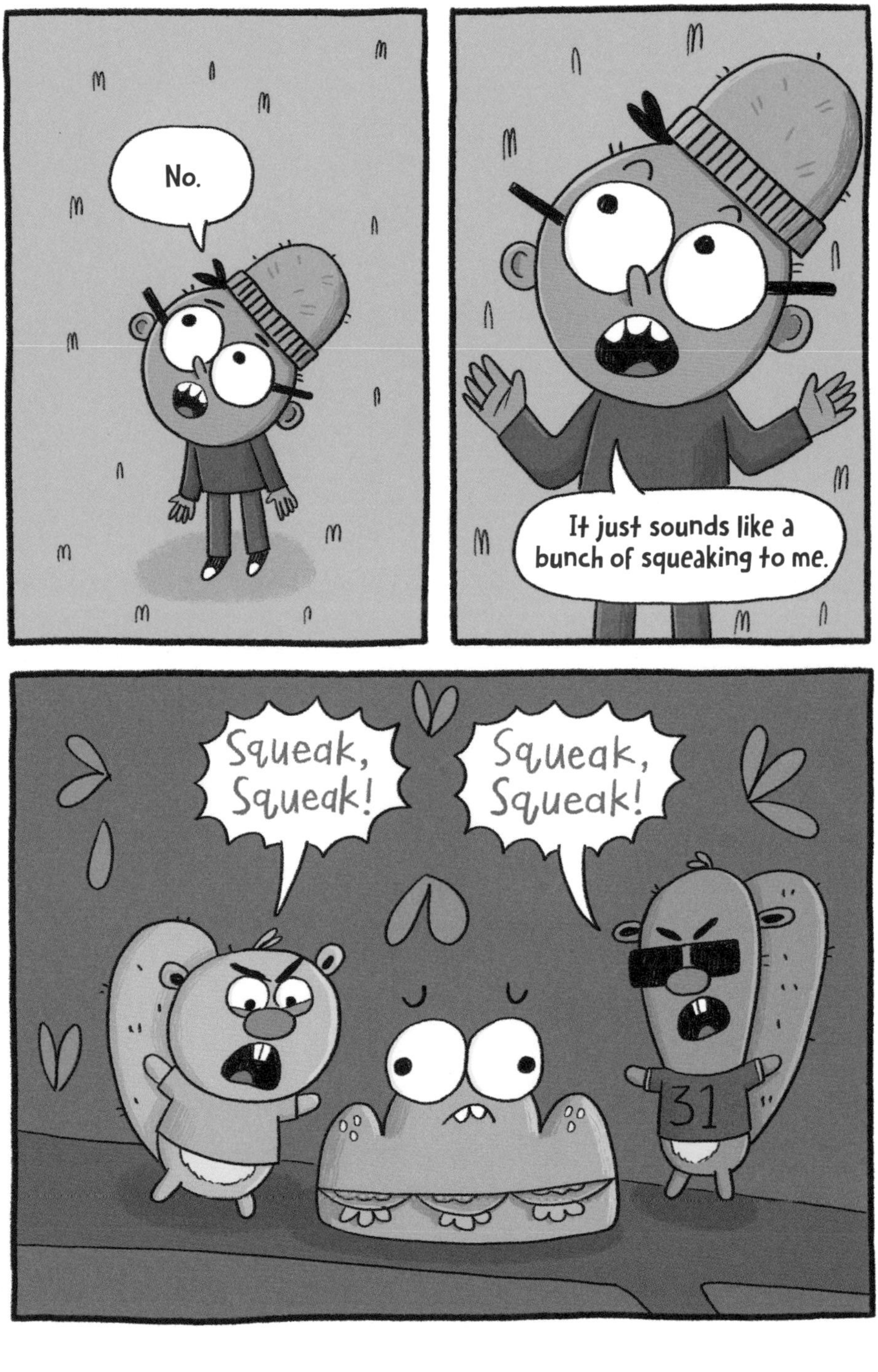
No.
It just sounds like a bunch of squeaking to me.
Squeak, Squeak!
Squeak, Squeak!
31

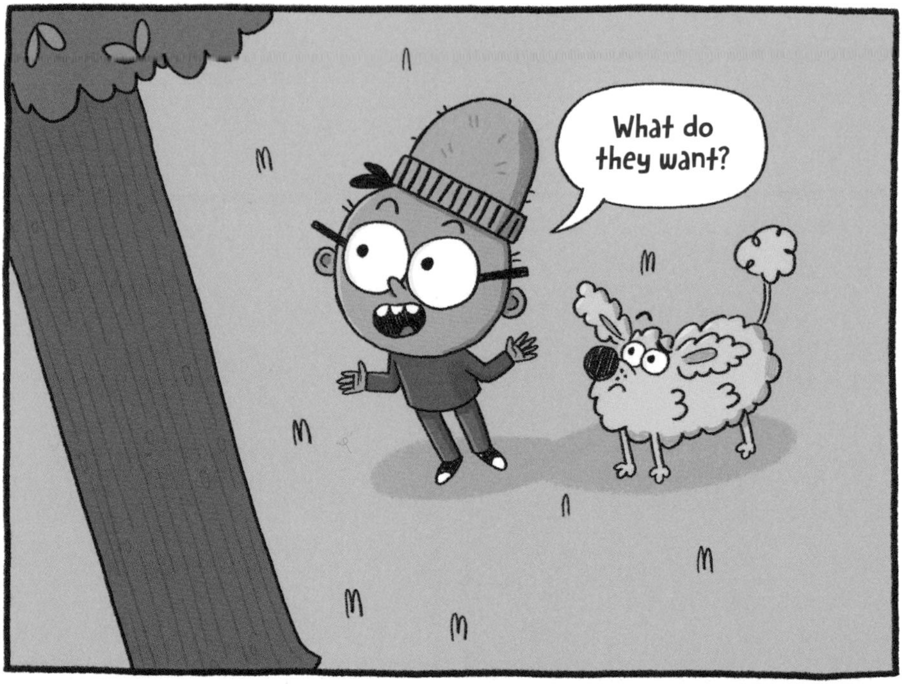
What do they want?

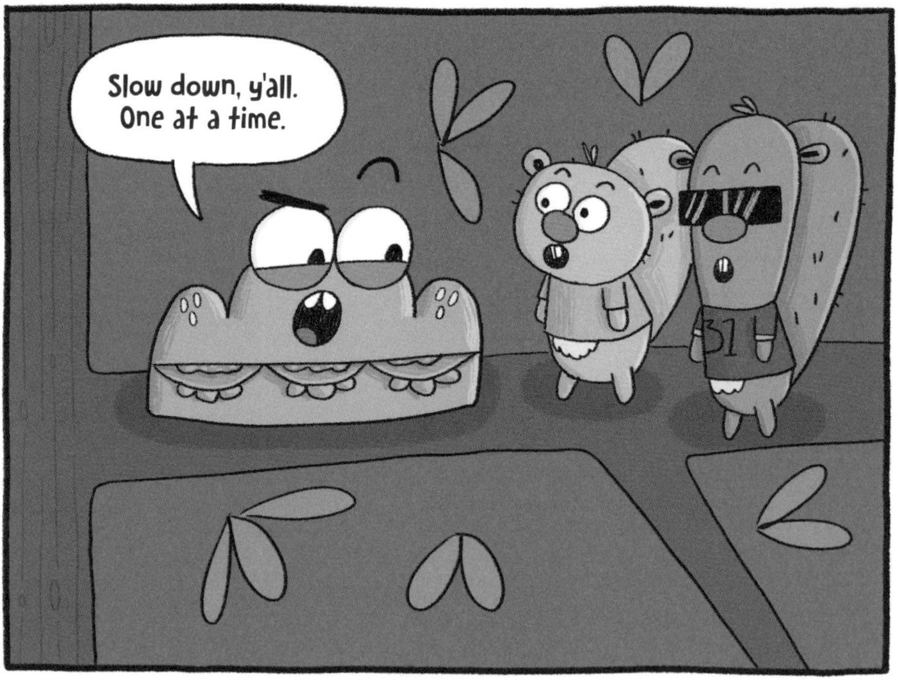
Slow down, y'all. One at a time.
31

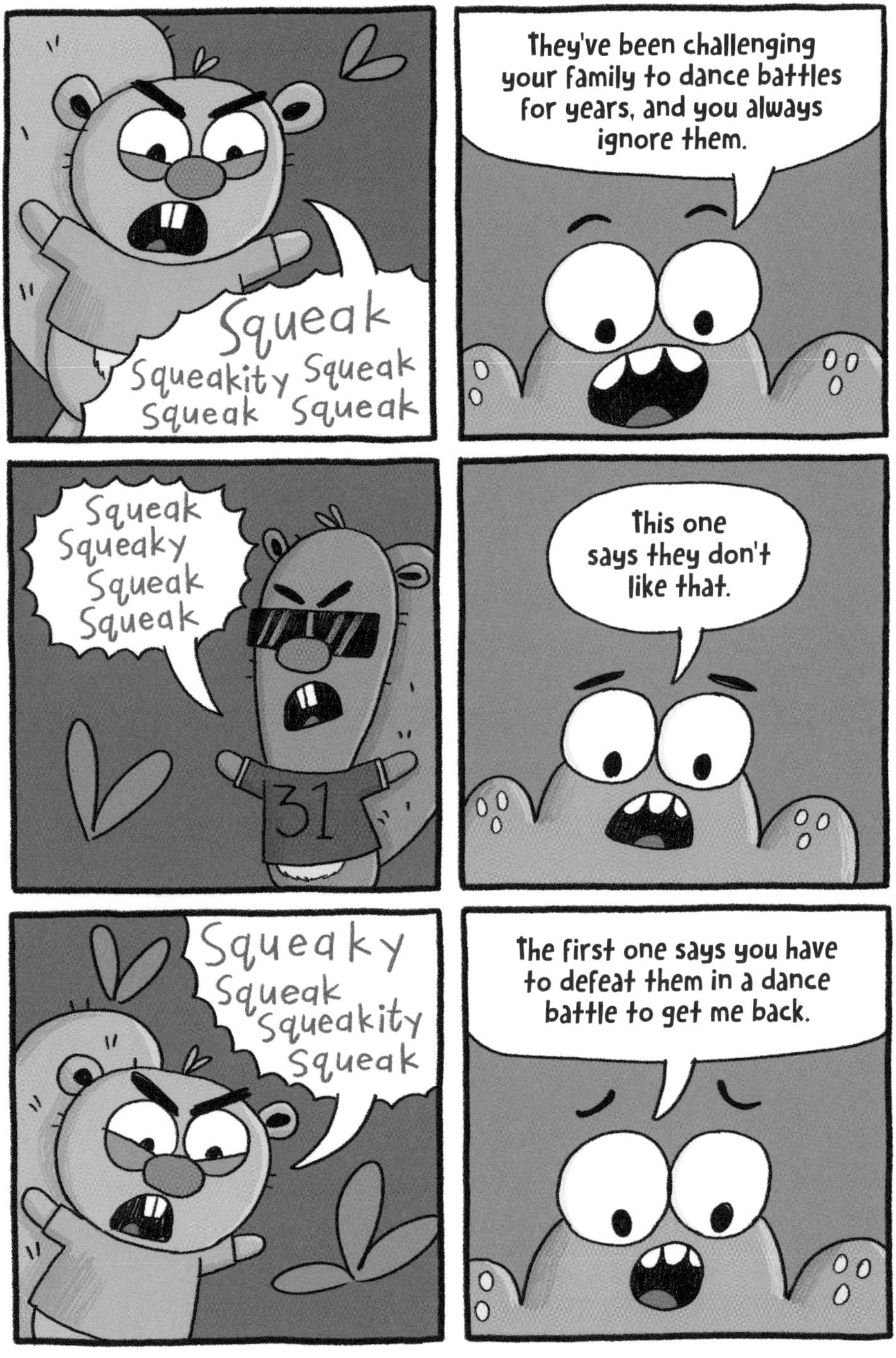
Squeak
Squeakity Squeak
squeak Squeak
They've been challenging your family to dance battles for years, and you always ignore them.
Squeak
Squeaky
Squeak
Squeak
31
This one says they don't like that.
Squeaky
Squeak
Squeakity
Squeak
The first one says you have to defeat them in a dance battle to get me back.

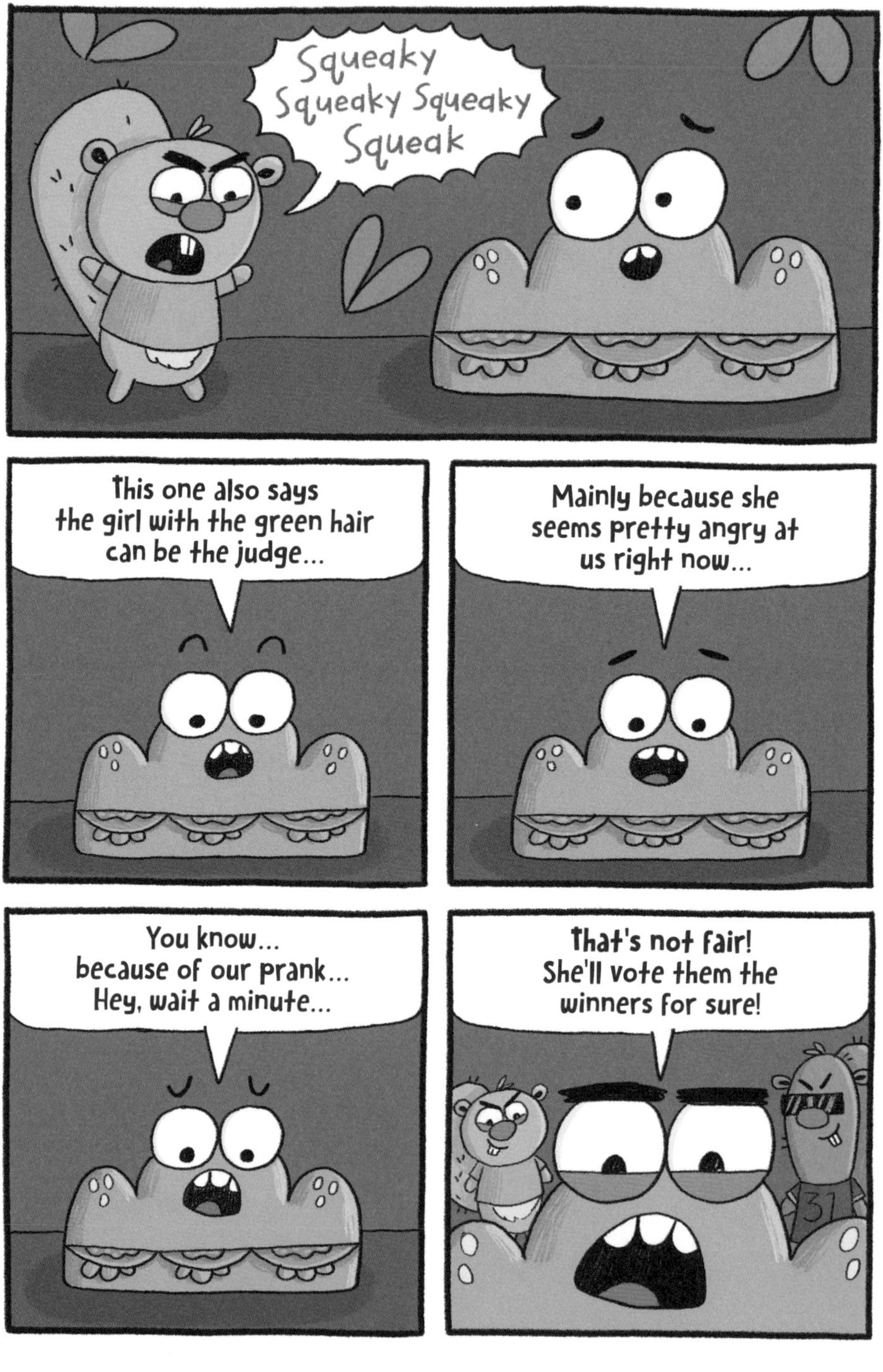
Squeaky Squeaky Squeaky Squeak
This one also says the girl with the green hair can be the judge...
Mainly because she seems pretty angry at us right now...
You know... because of our prank... Hey, wait a minute...
That's not fair! She'll vote them the winners for sure!
31

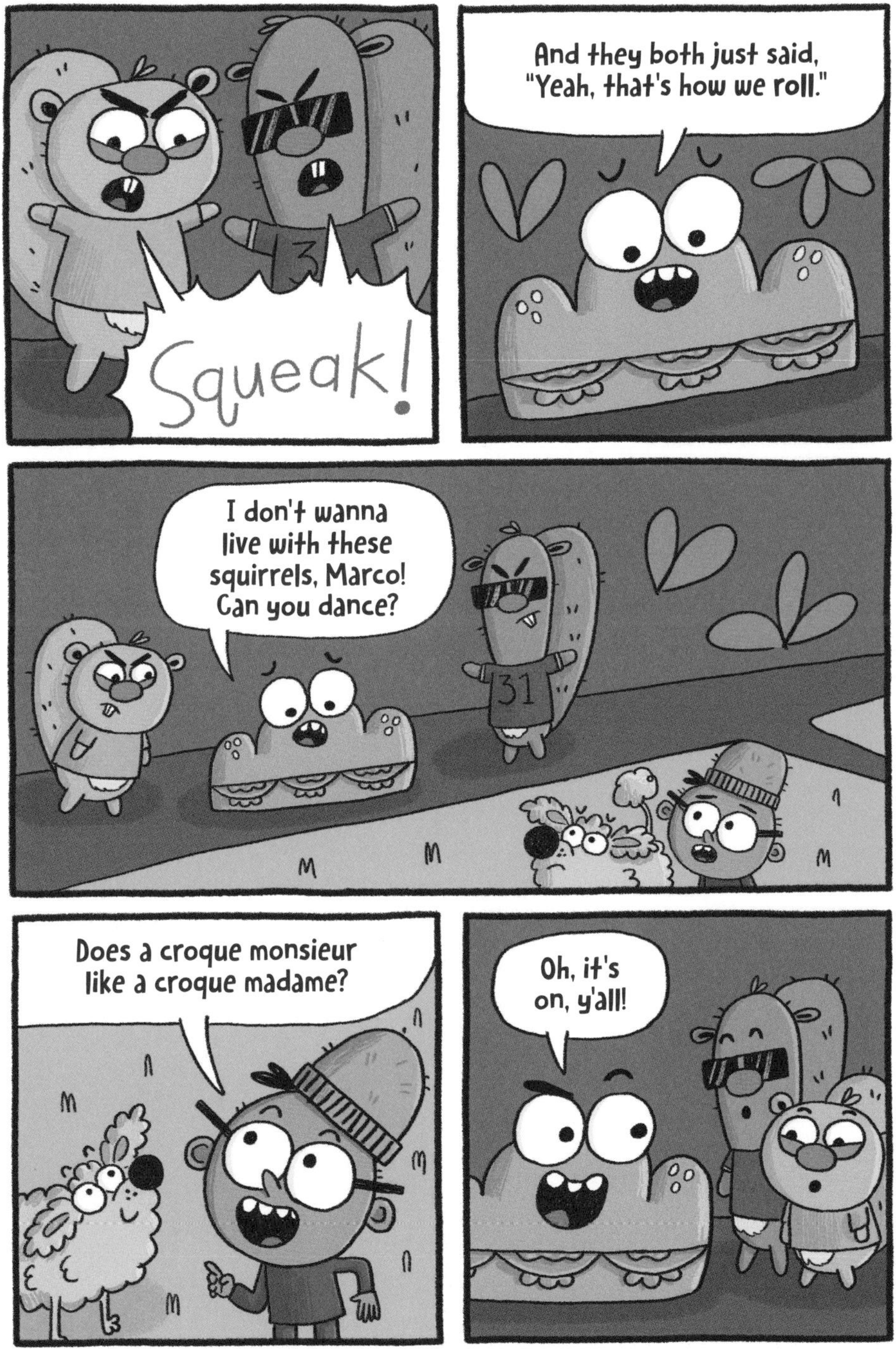
Squeak!
And they both just said, "Yeah, that's how we roll."
I don't wanna live with these squirrels, Marco! Can you dance?
31
Does a croque monsieur like a croque madame?
Oh, it's on, y'all!

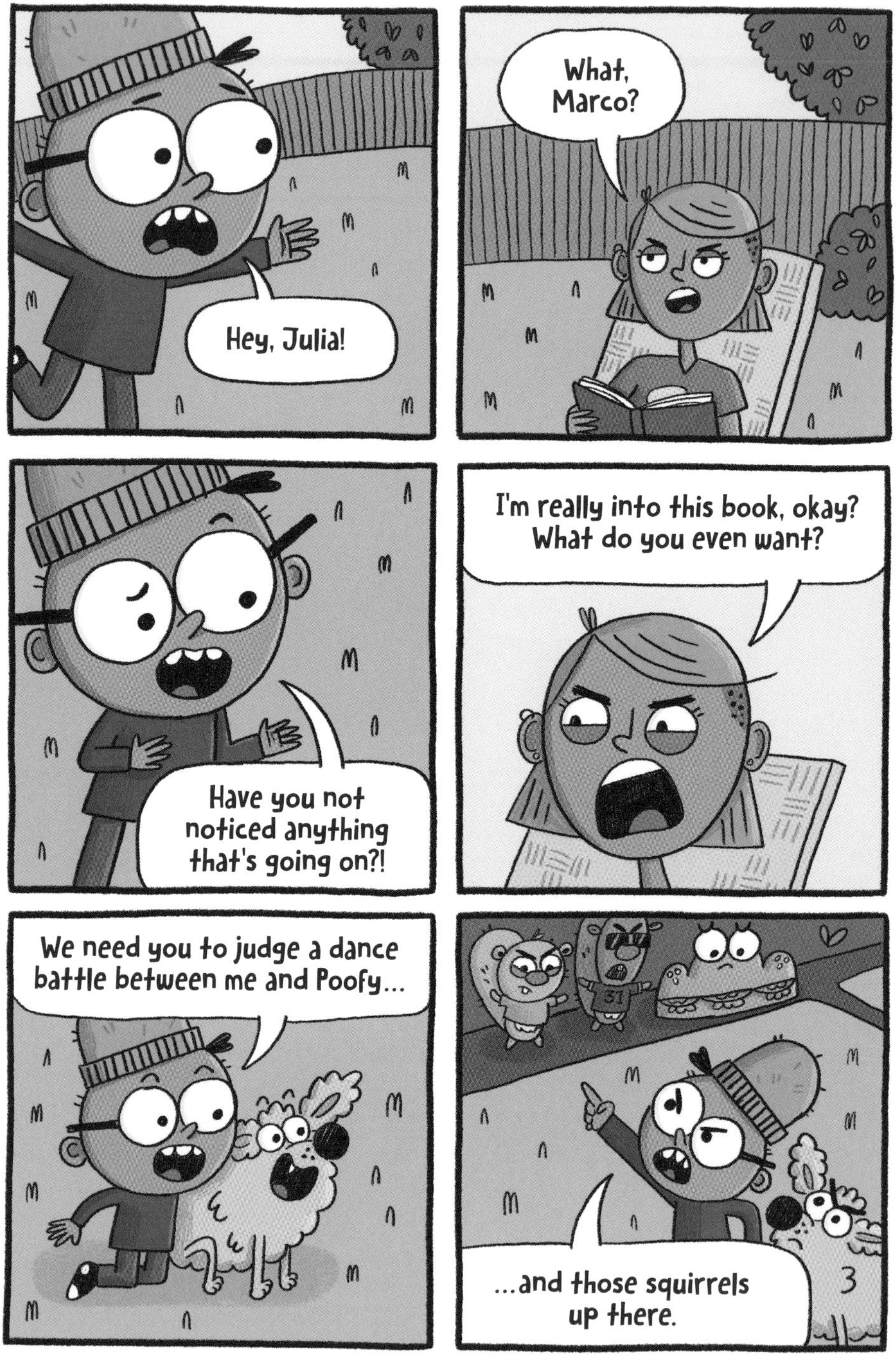
Hey, Julia!
What, Marco?
Have you not noticed anything that's going on?!
I'm really into this book, okay? What do you even want?
We need you to judge a dance battle between me and Poofy...
...and those squirrels up there.
3

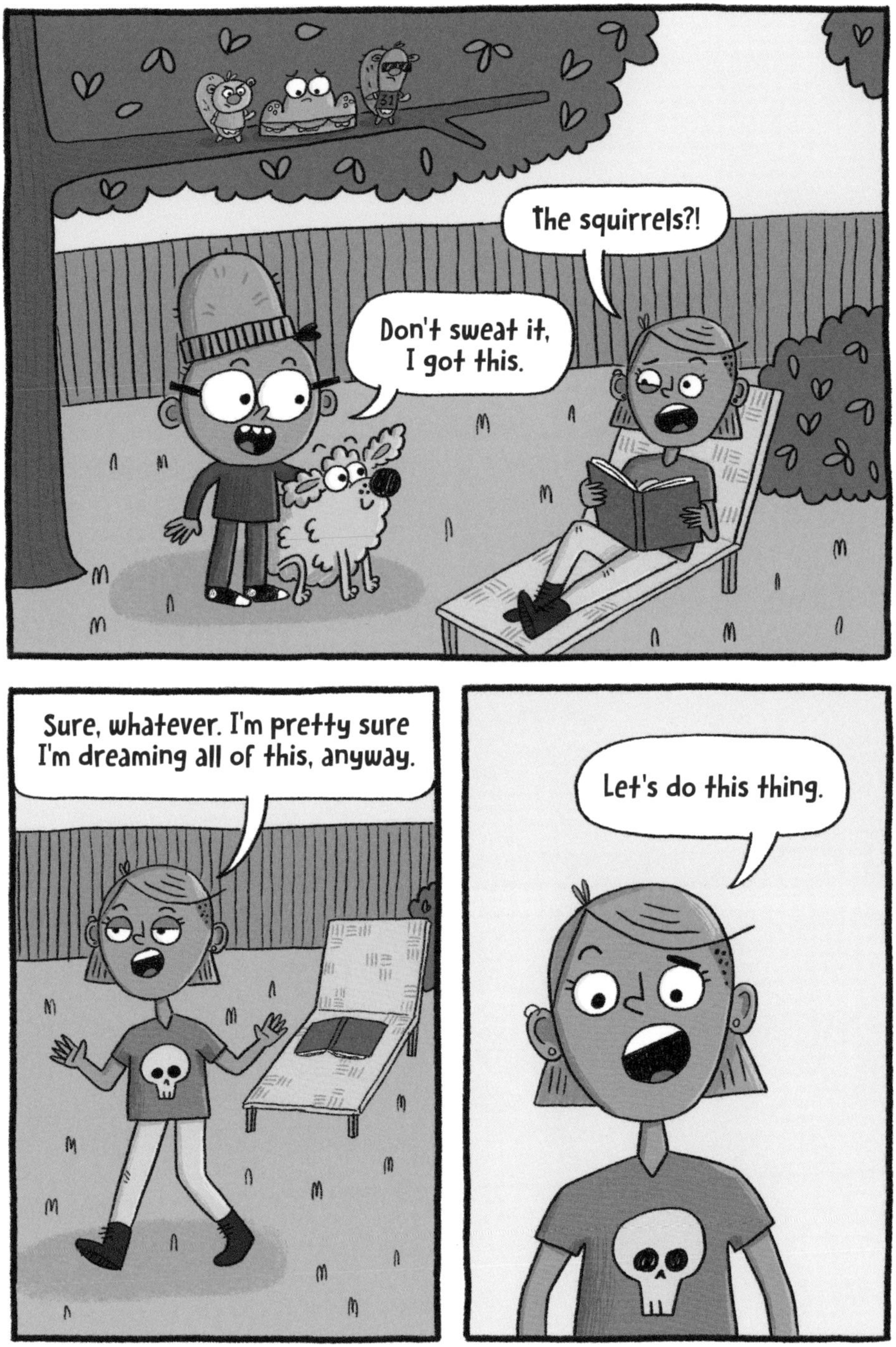
The squirrels?!
Don't sweat it, I got this.
Sure, whatever. I'm pretty sure I'm dreaming all of this, anyway.
Let's do this thing.

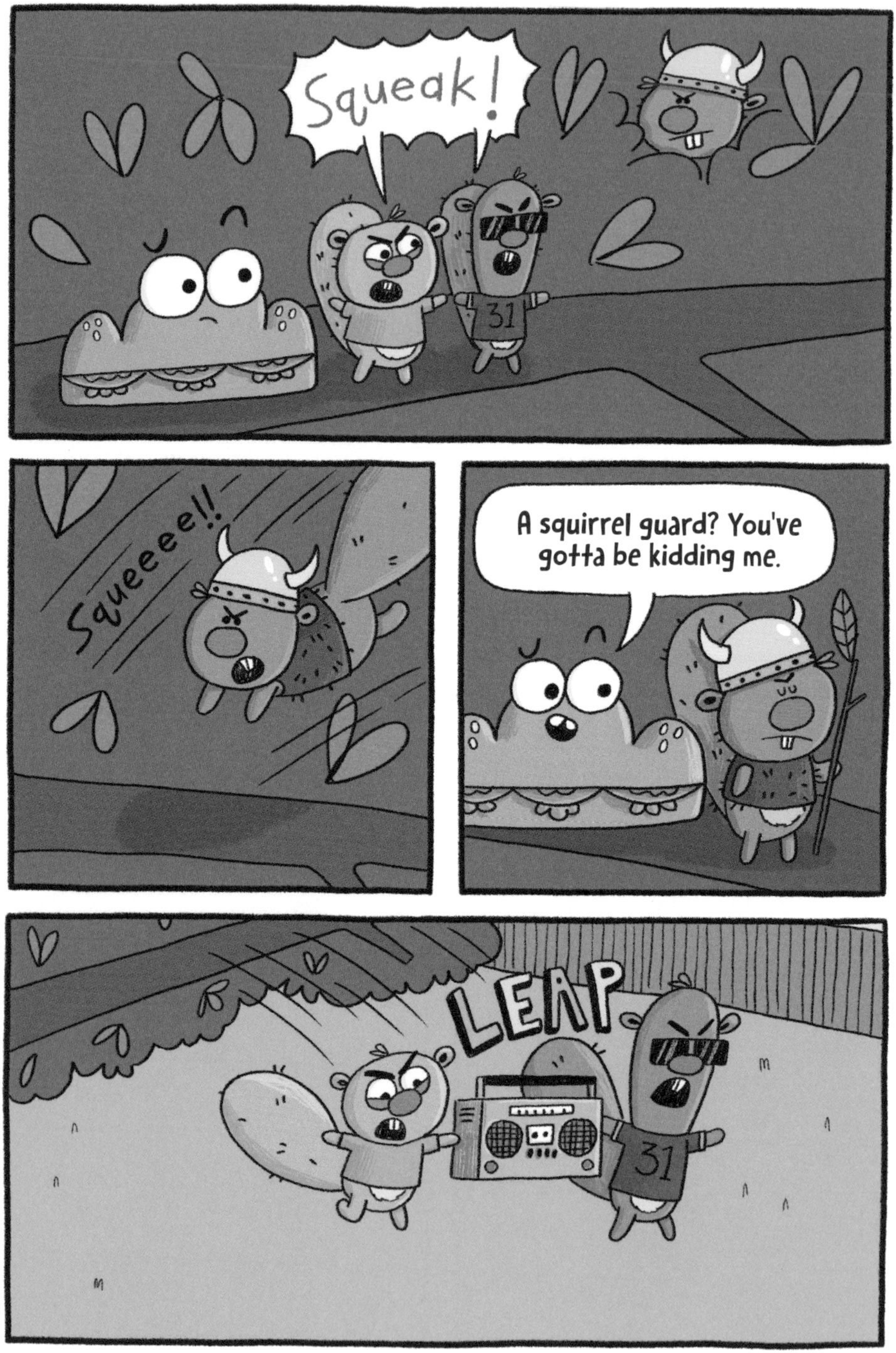

Squeak!
Squeeeee!!
A squirrel guard? You've gotta be kidding me.
LEAP
31

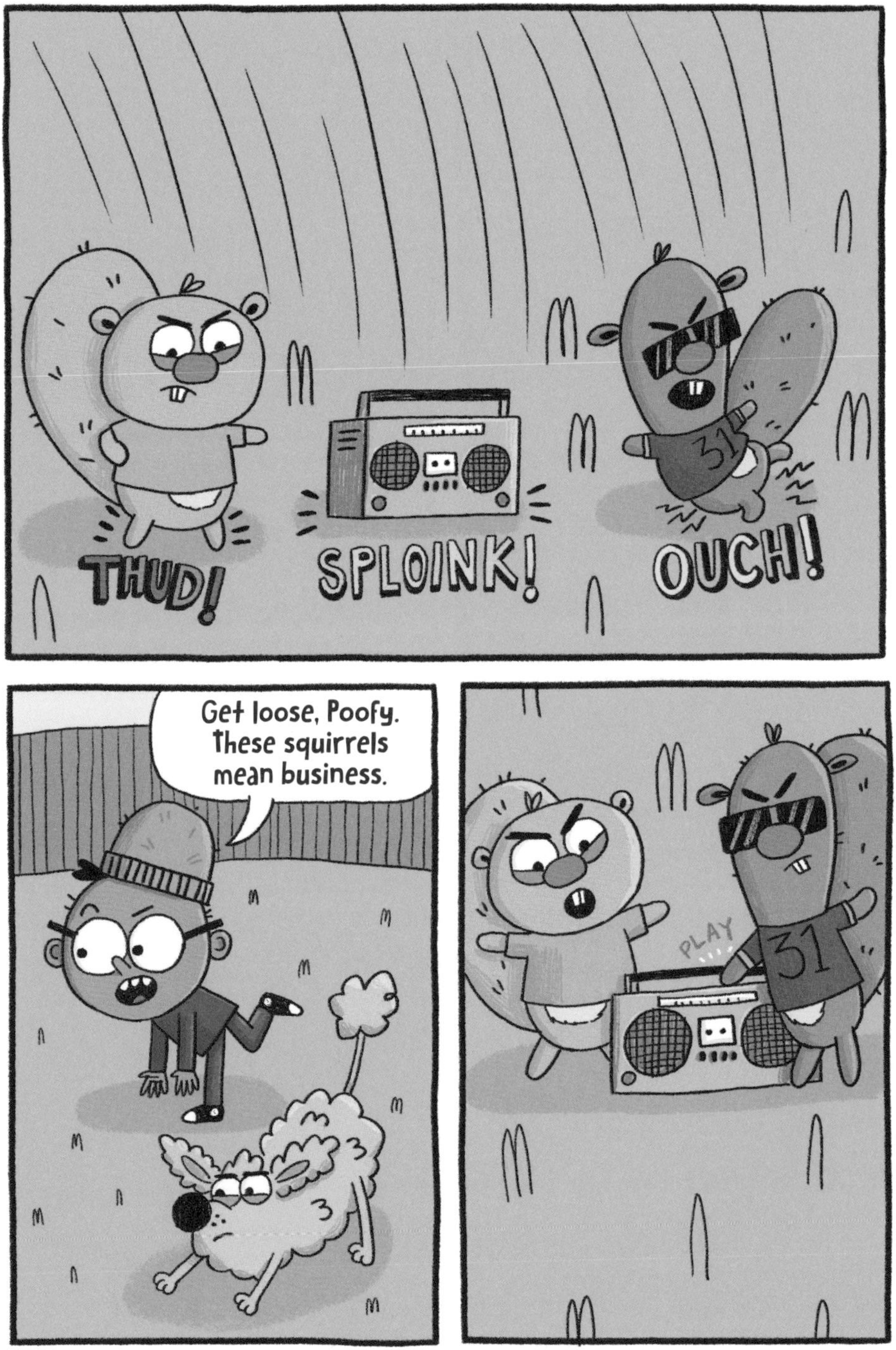
THUD!
SPLOINK!
OUCH!
Get loose, Poofy. These squirrels mean business.
PLAY

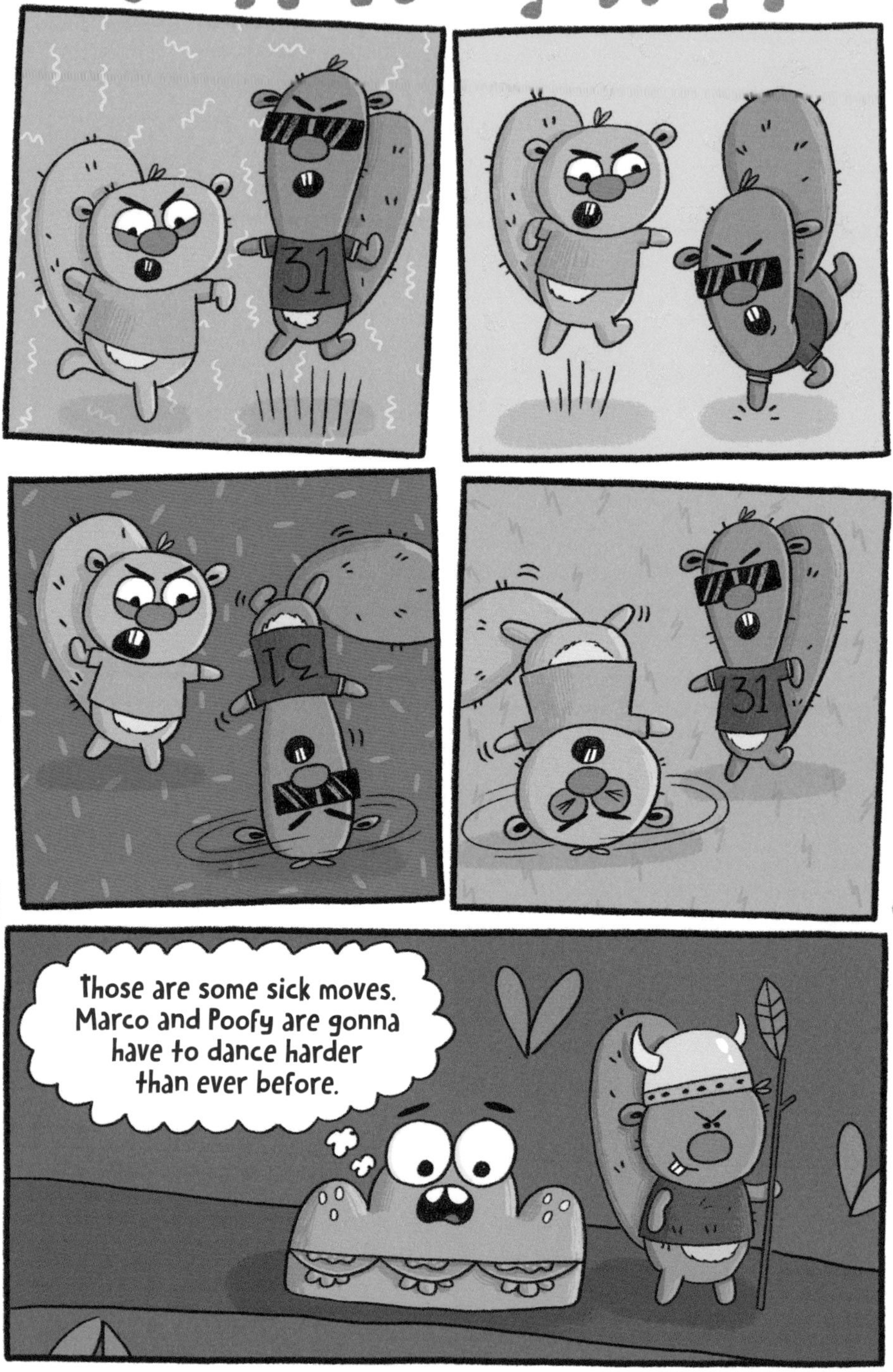

31
31
31
31
Those are some sick moves. Marco and Poofy are gonna have to dance harder than ever before.

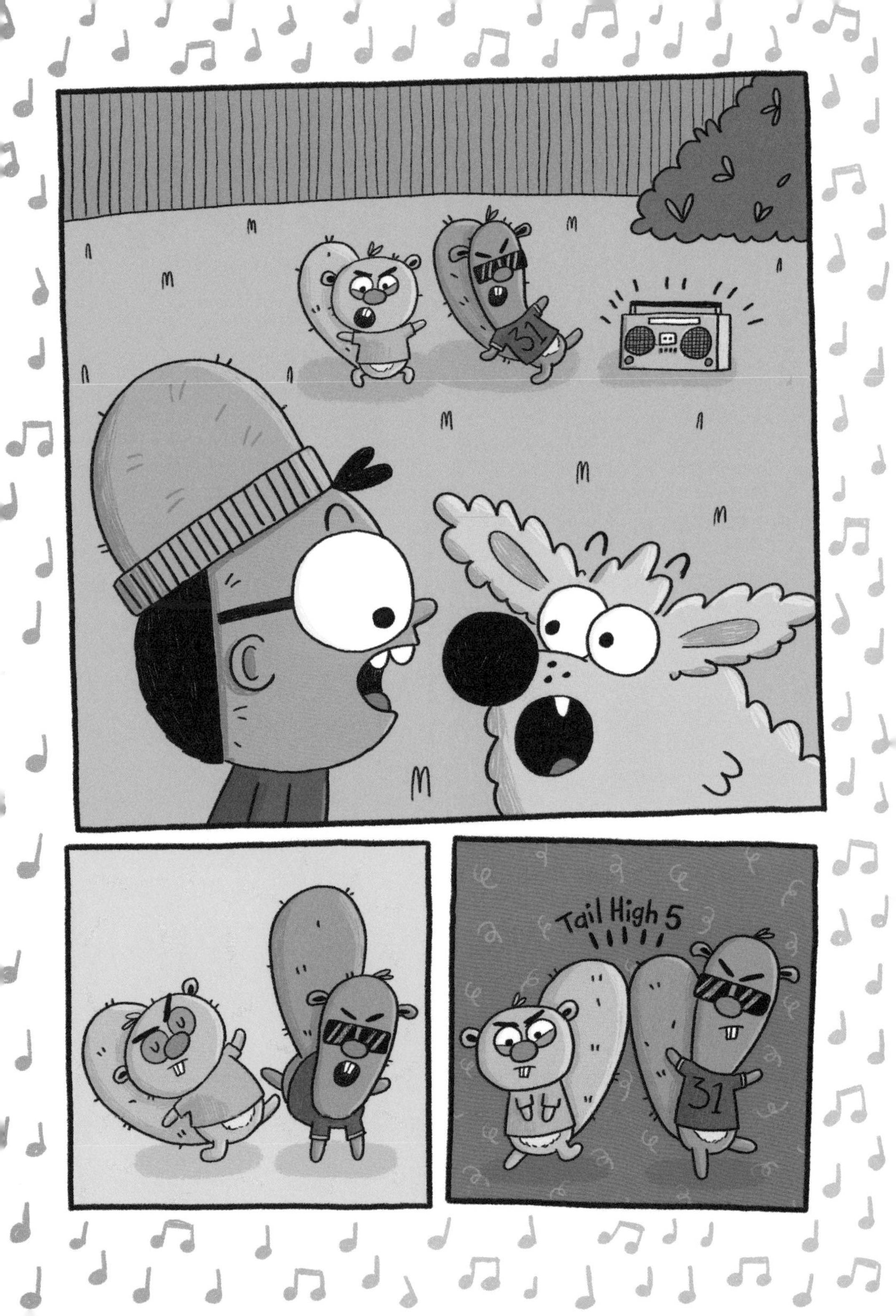
Tail High 5

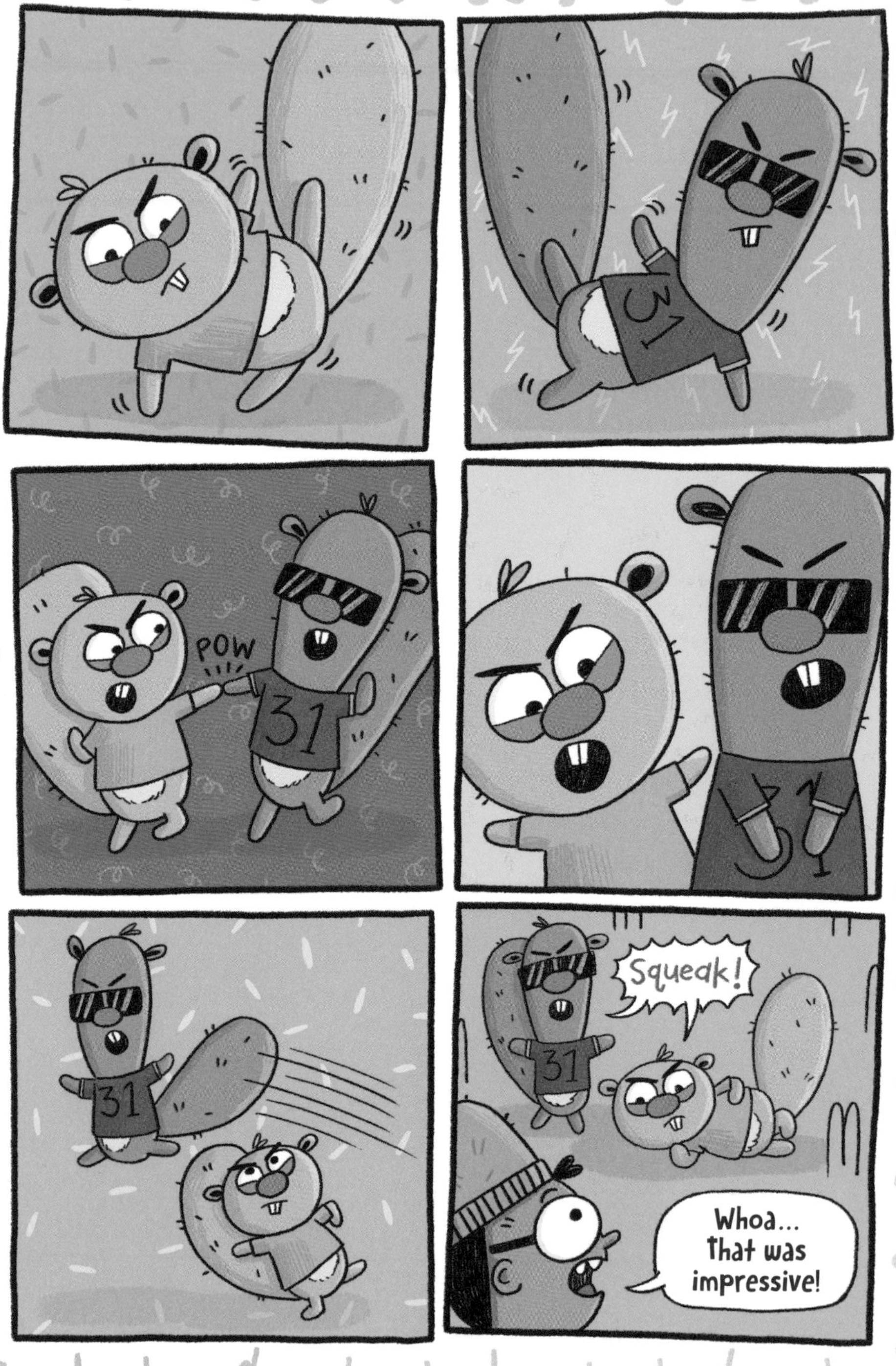
POW
Squeak!
Whoa... That was impressive!

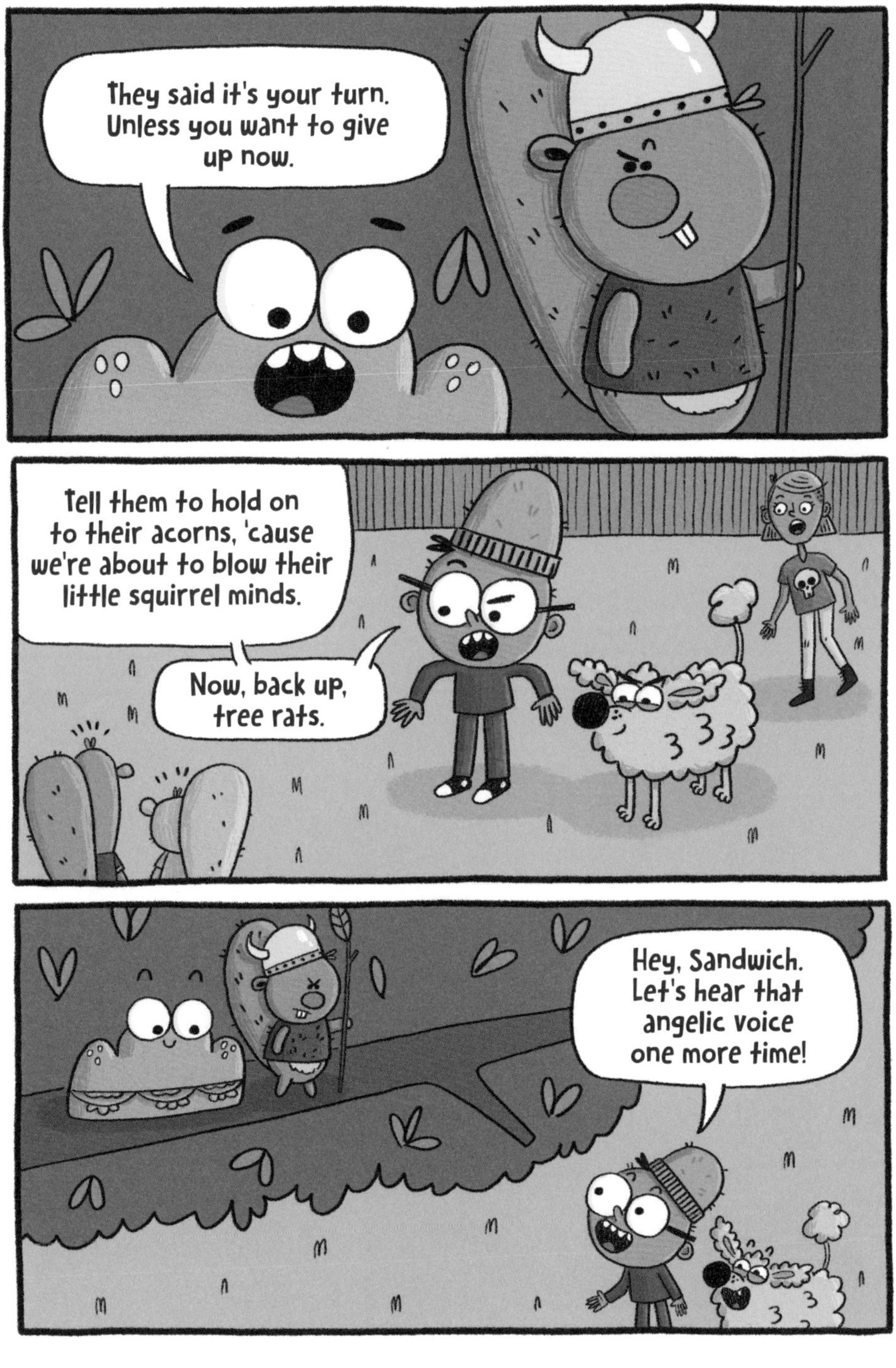
They said it's your turn. Unless you want to give up now.
Tell them to hold on to their acorns, 'cause we're about to blow their little squirrel minds.
Now, back up, tree rats.
Hey, Sandwich. Let's hear that angelic voice one more time!

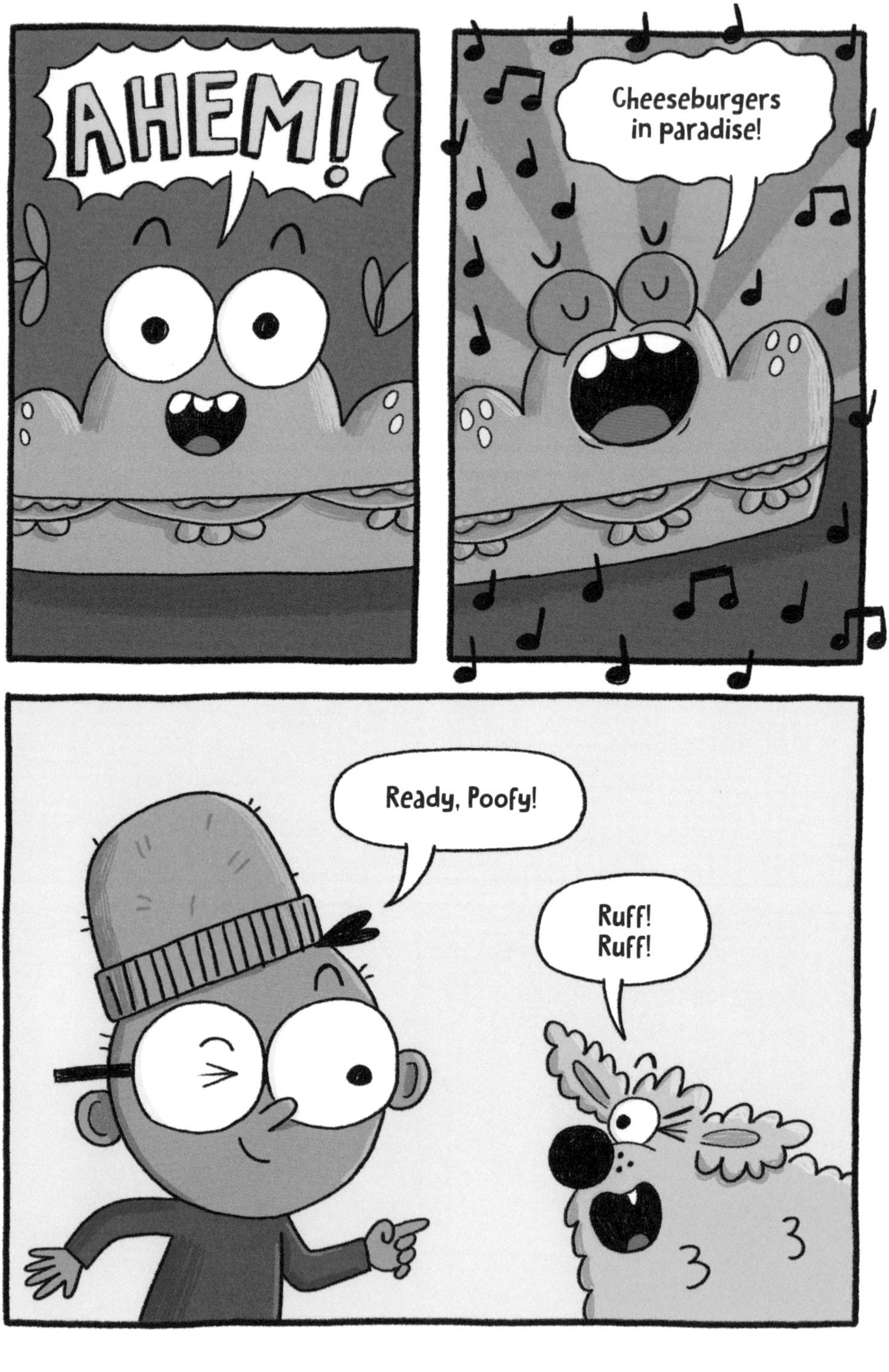
AHEM!
Cheeseburgers in paradise!
Ready, Poofy!
Ruff! Ruff!

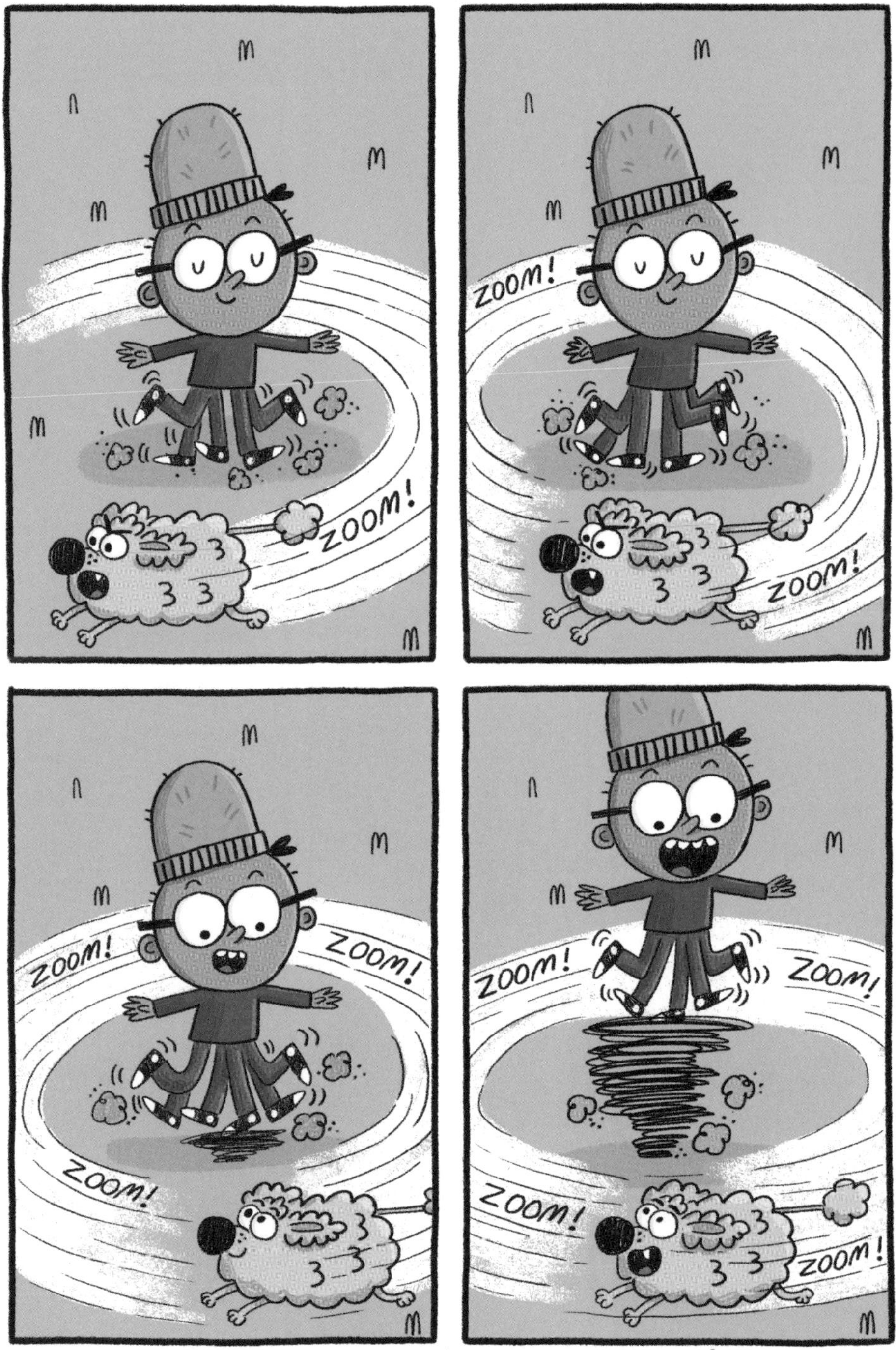
ZOOM!
ZOOM!
ZOOM!
ZOOM!
ZOOM!
ZOOM!
ZOOM!
ZOOM!
ZOOM!
ZOOM!
ZOOM!

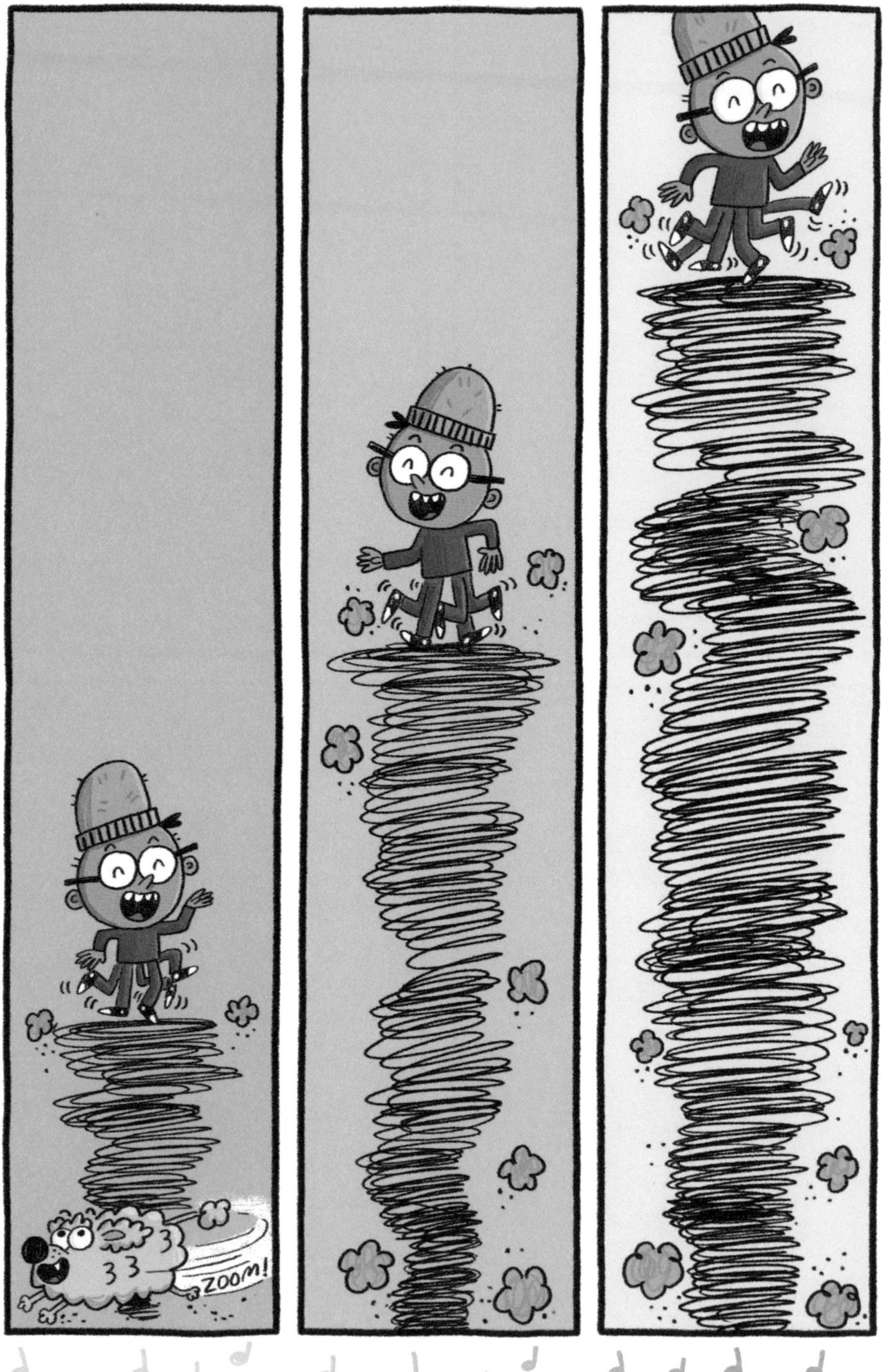
ZOOM!

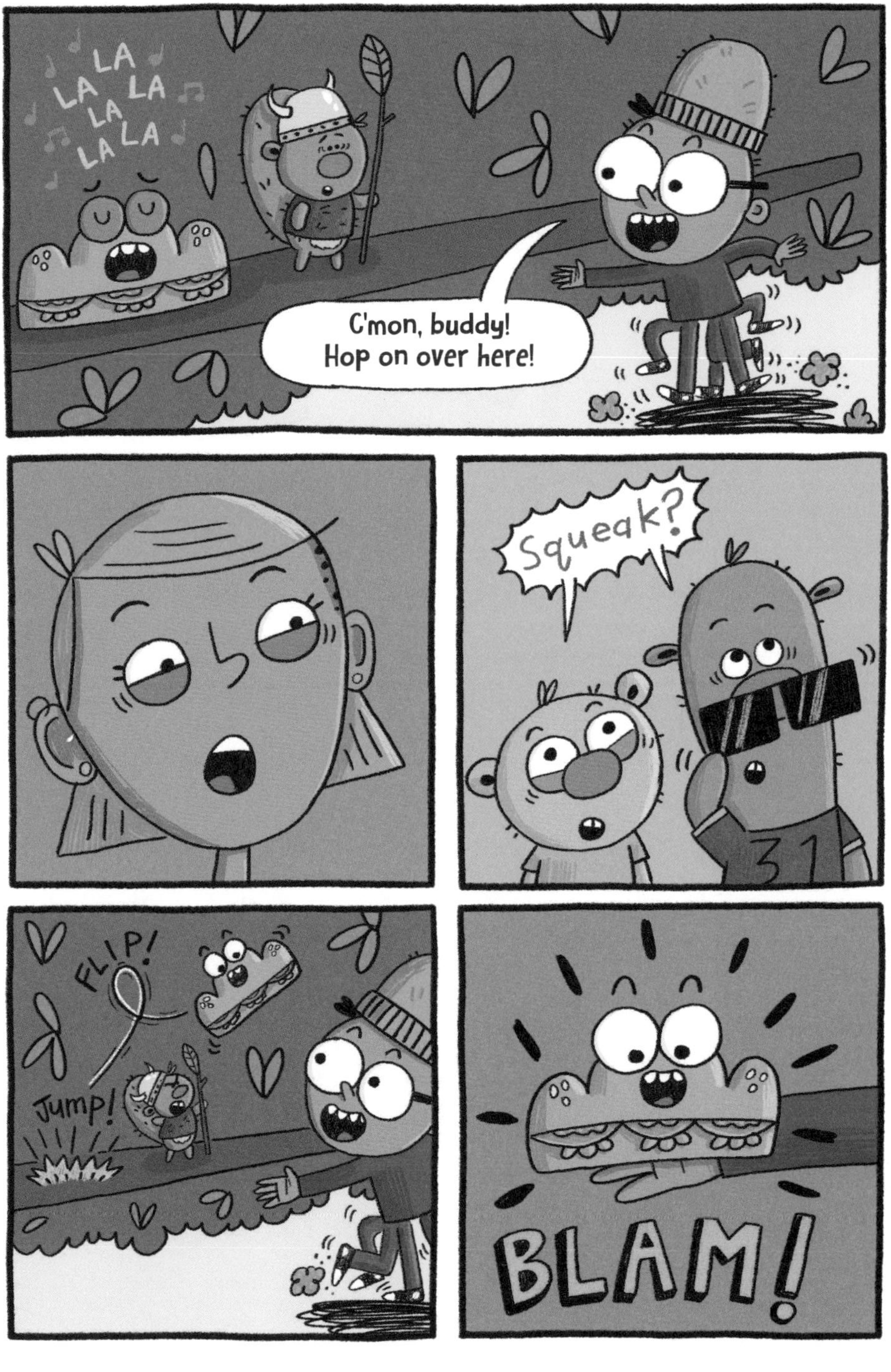
LA LA LA LA LA LA
C'mon, buddy!
Hop on over here!
Squeak?
FLIP!
JUMP!
BLAM!

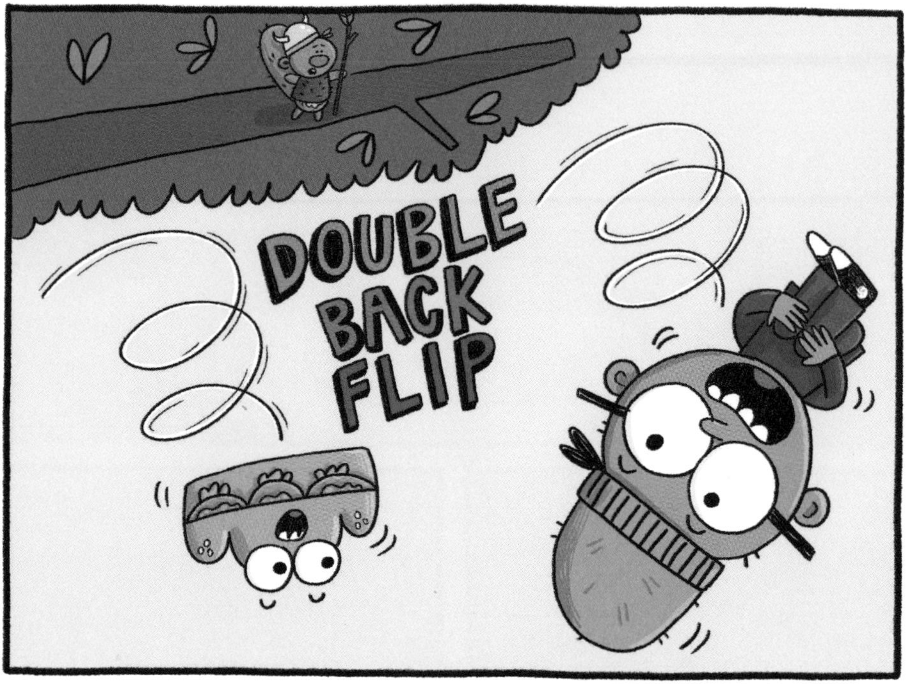
DOUBLE BACK FLIP

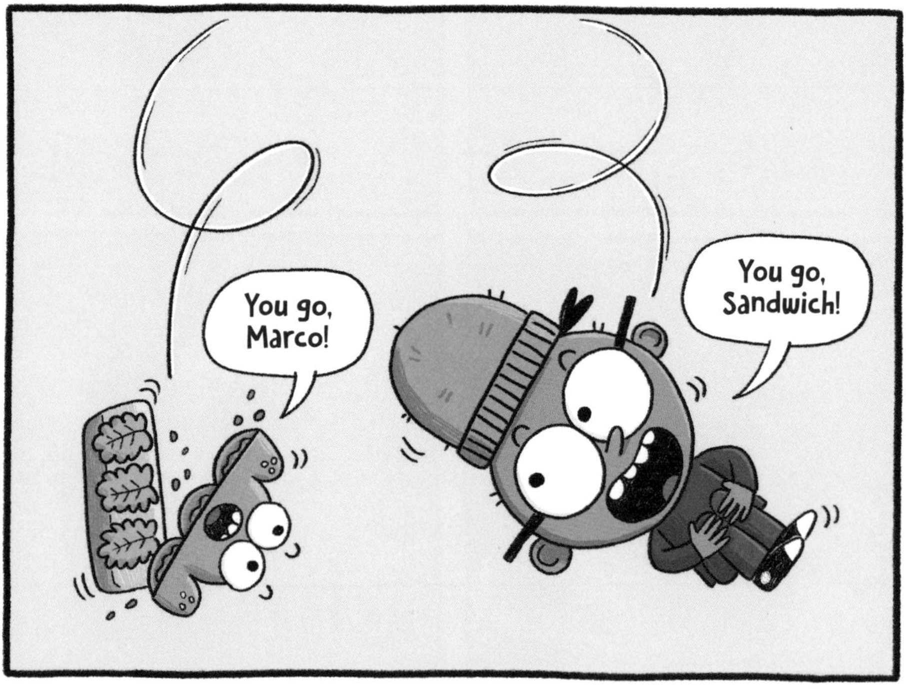
You go, Marco!
You go, Sandwich!

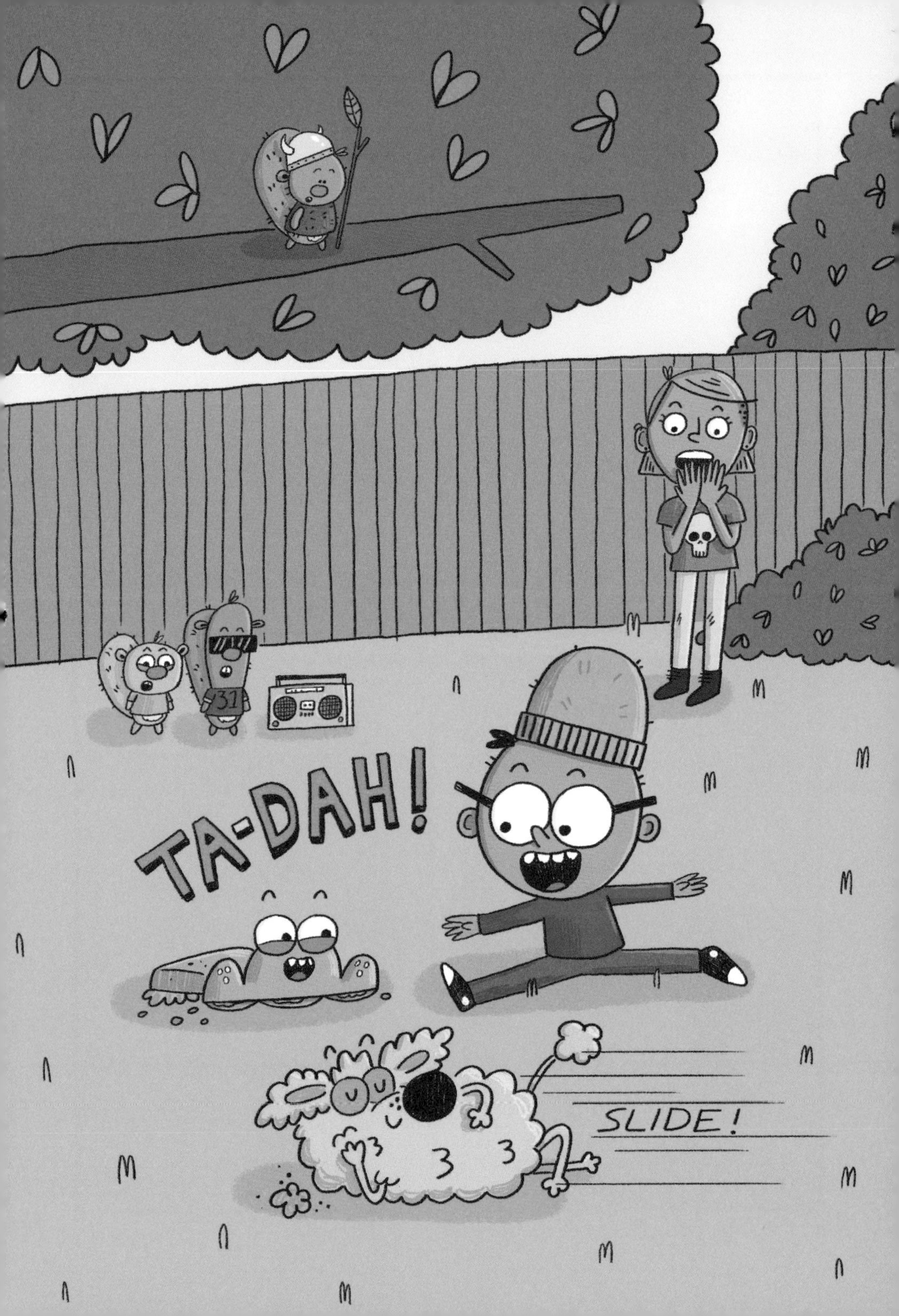
TA-DAH!
SLIDE!

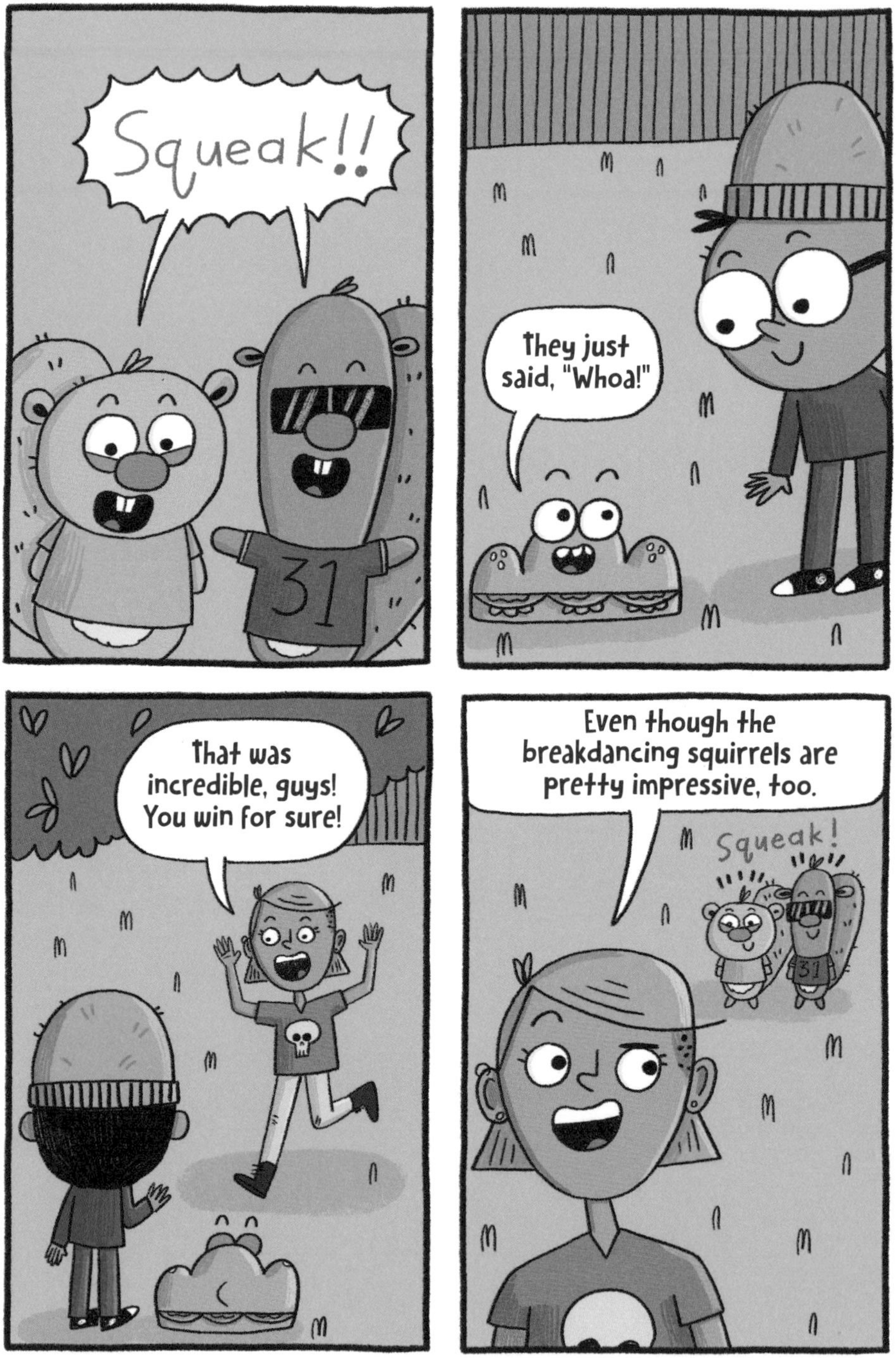
Squeak!!
They just said, "Whoa!"
That was incredible, guys! You win for sure!
Even though the breakdancing squirrels are pretty impressive, too.
Squeak!

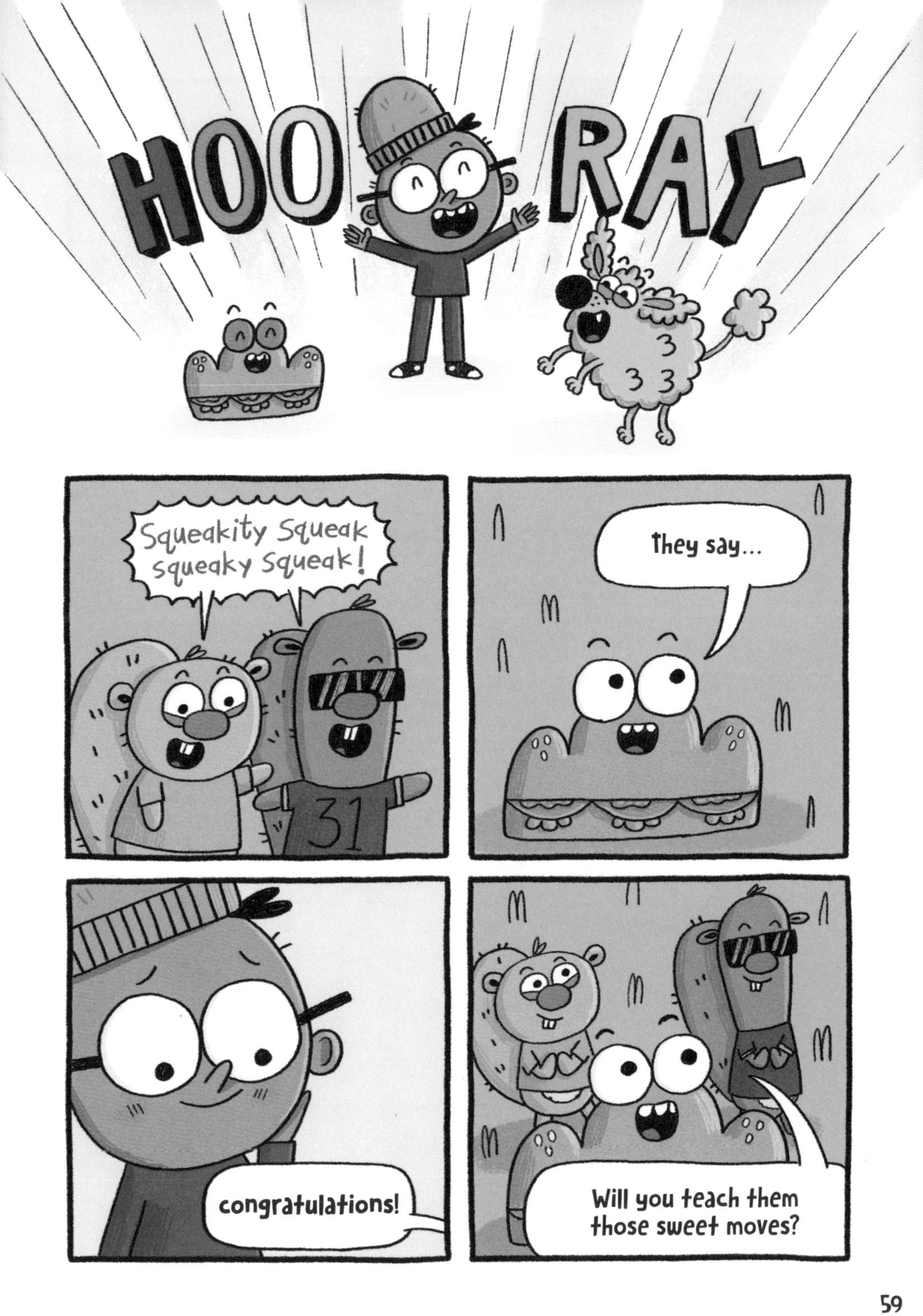
HOOORAY
Squeakity Squeak squeaky Squeak!
they say...
congratulations!
Will you teach them those sweet moves?

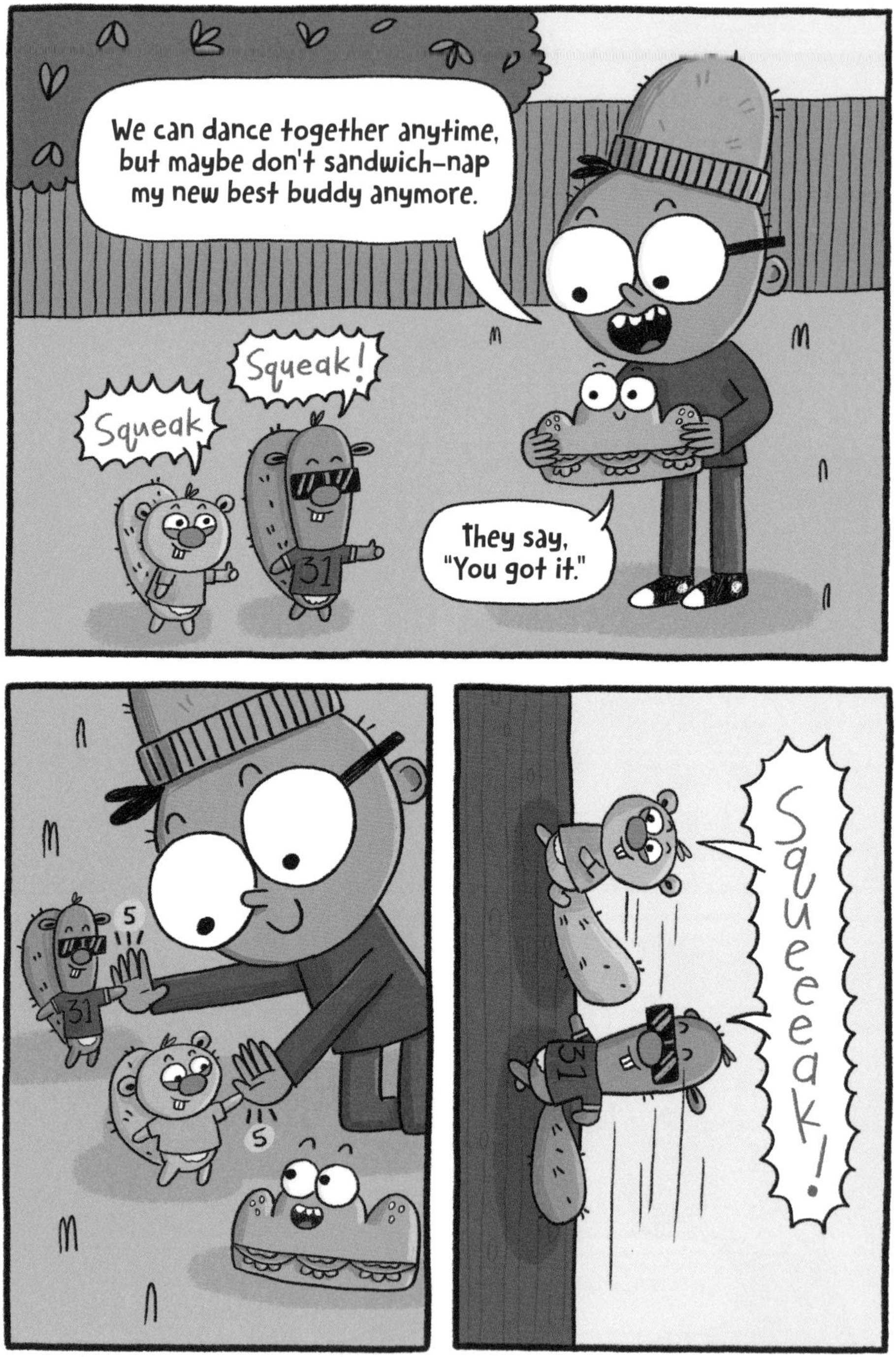
We can dance together anytime, but maybe don't sandwich-nap my new best buddy anymore.
Squeak
Squeak!
They say, "You got it."
5
5
Squeeeeak!

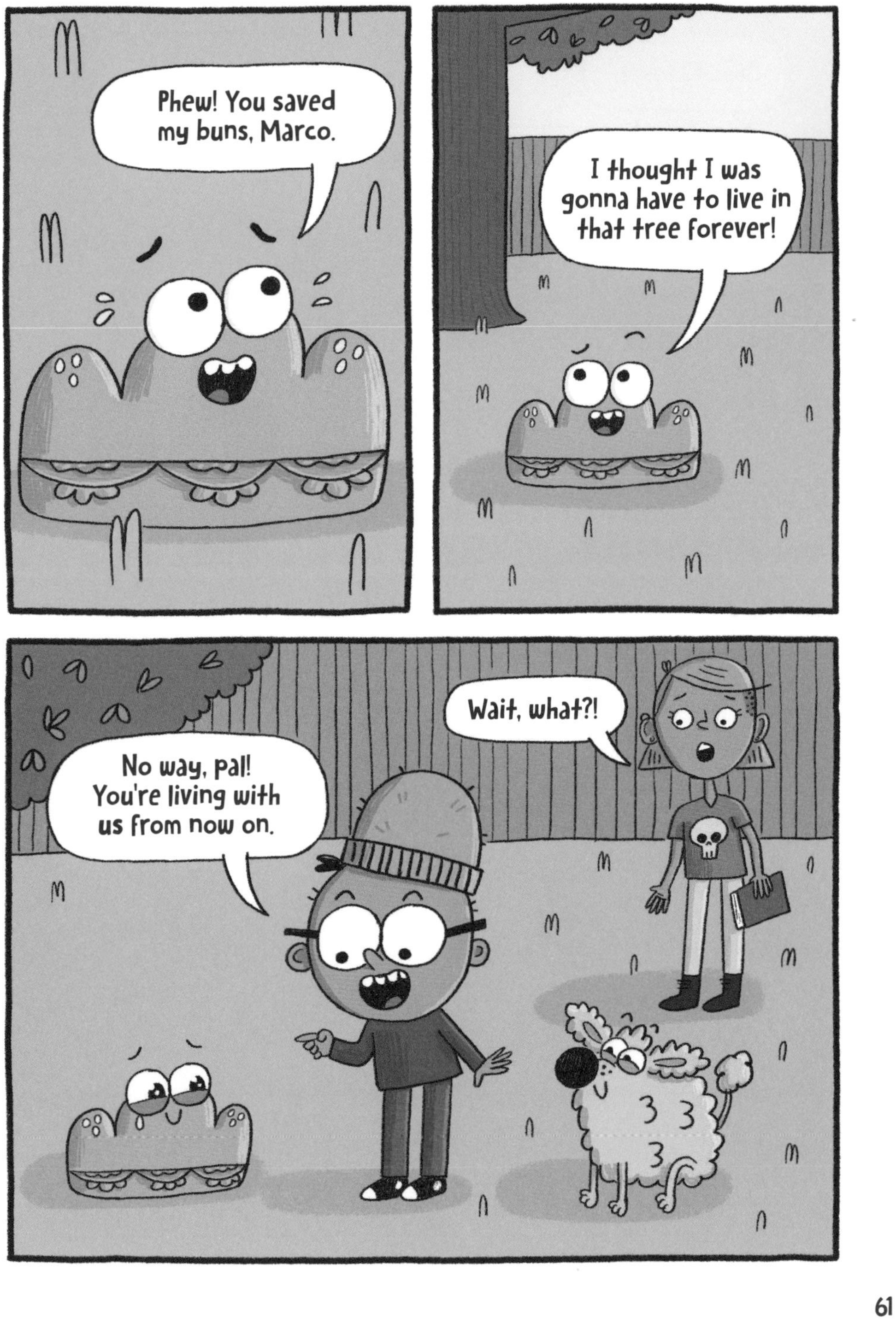
Phew! You saved my buns, Marco.
I thought I was gonna have to live in that tree forever!
No way, pal! You're living with us from now on.
Wait, what?!

Oh, whatever.
Just keep him out of my room.
And don't serve him to me for lunch anymore, either!
Speaking of lunch... that dance battle got me extra hungry.
Not for a sandwich, I hope!

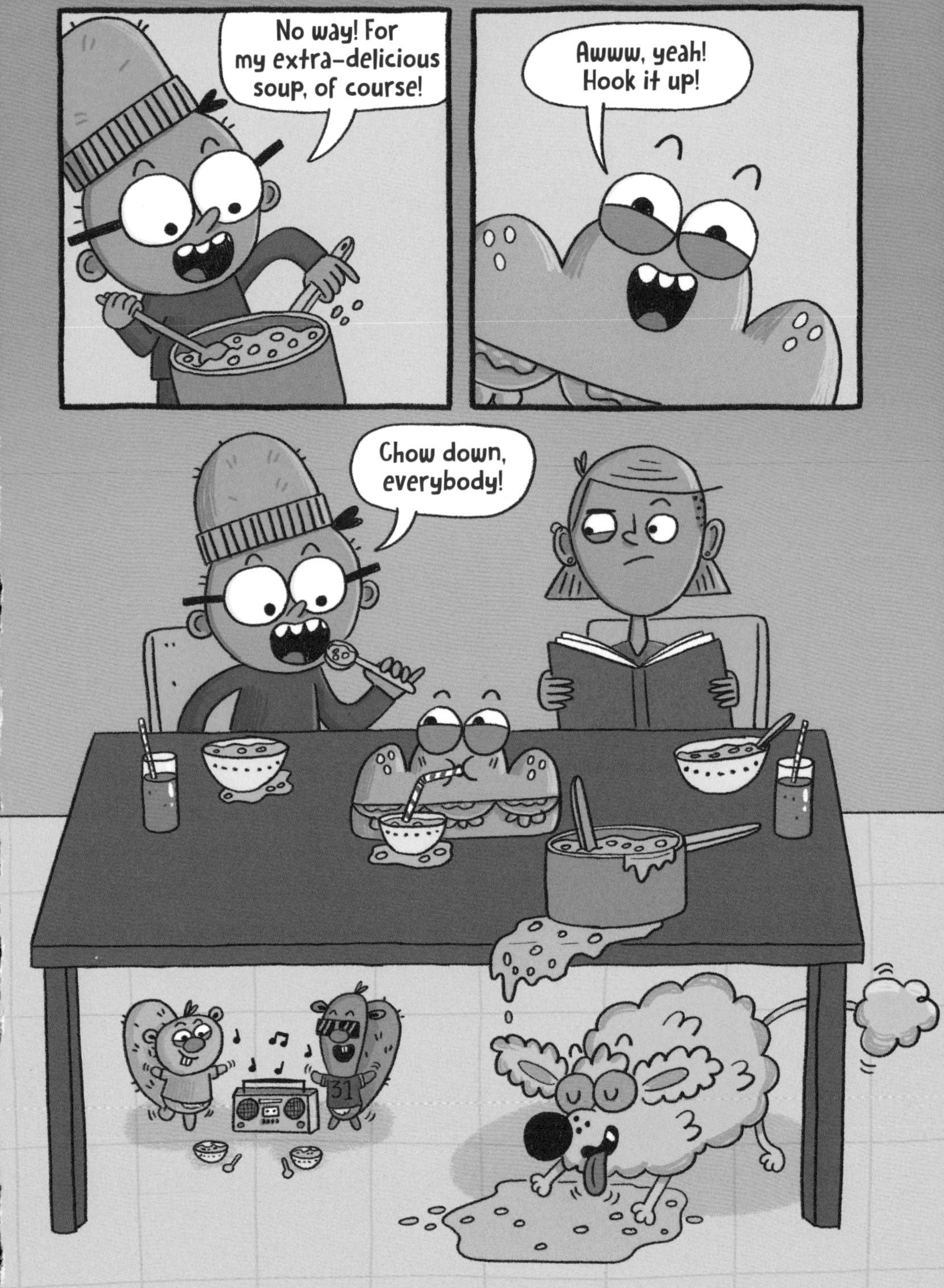
No way! For my extra-delicious soup, of course!
Awww, yeah! Hook it up!
Chow down, everybody!
31

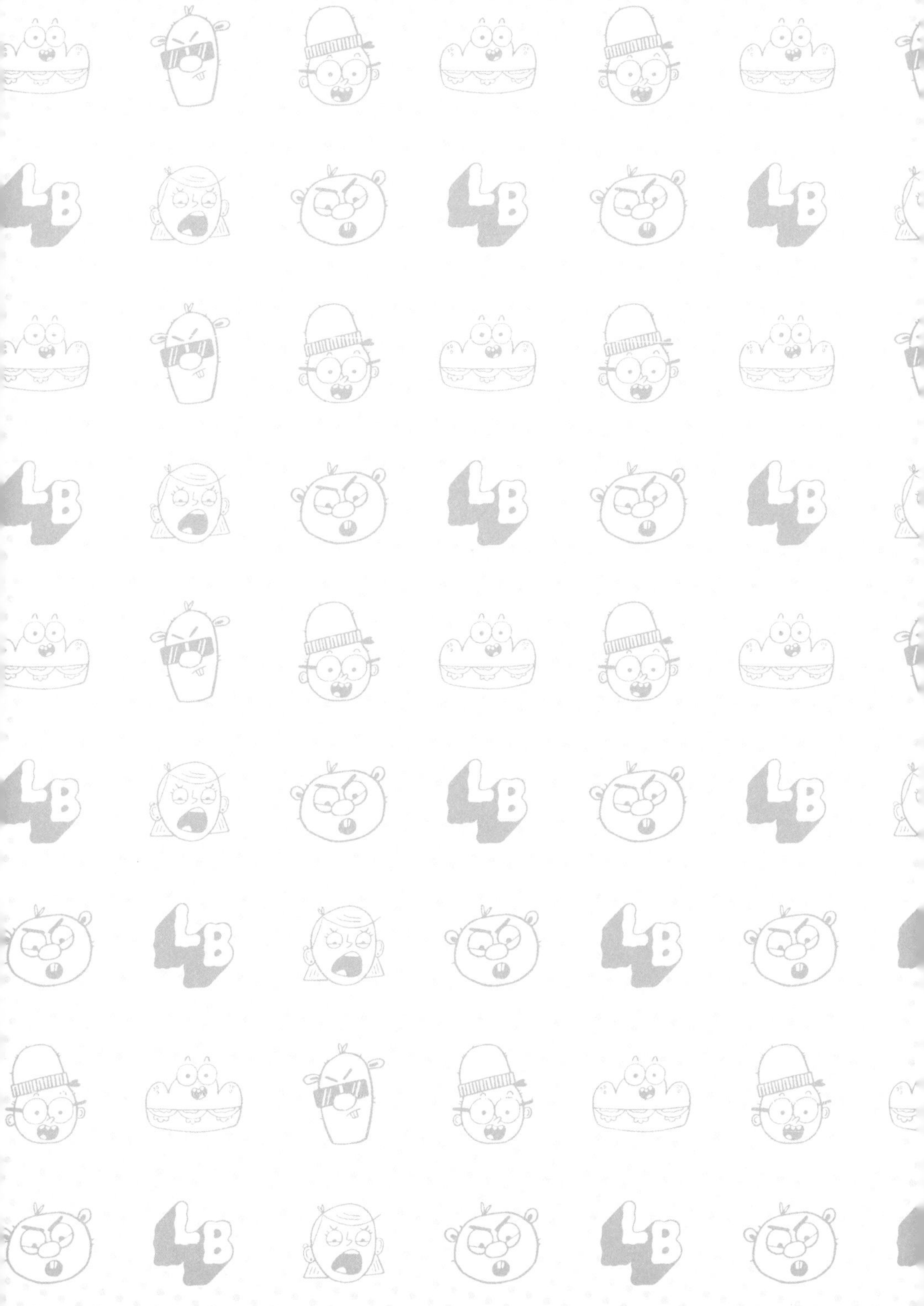

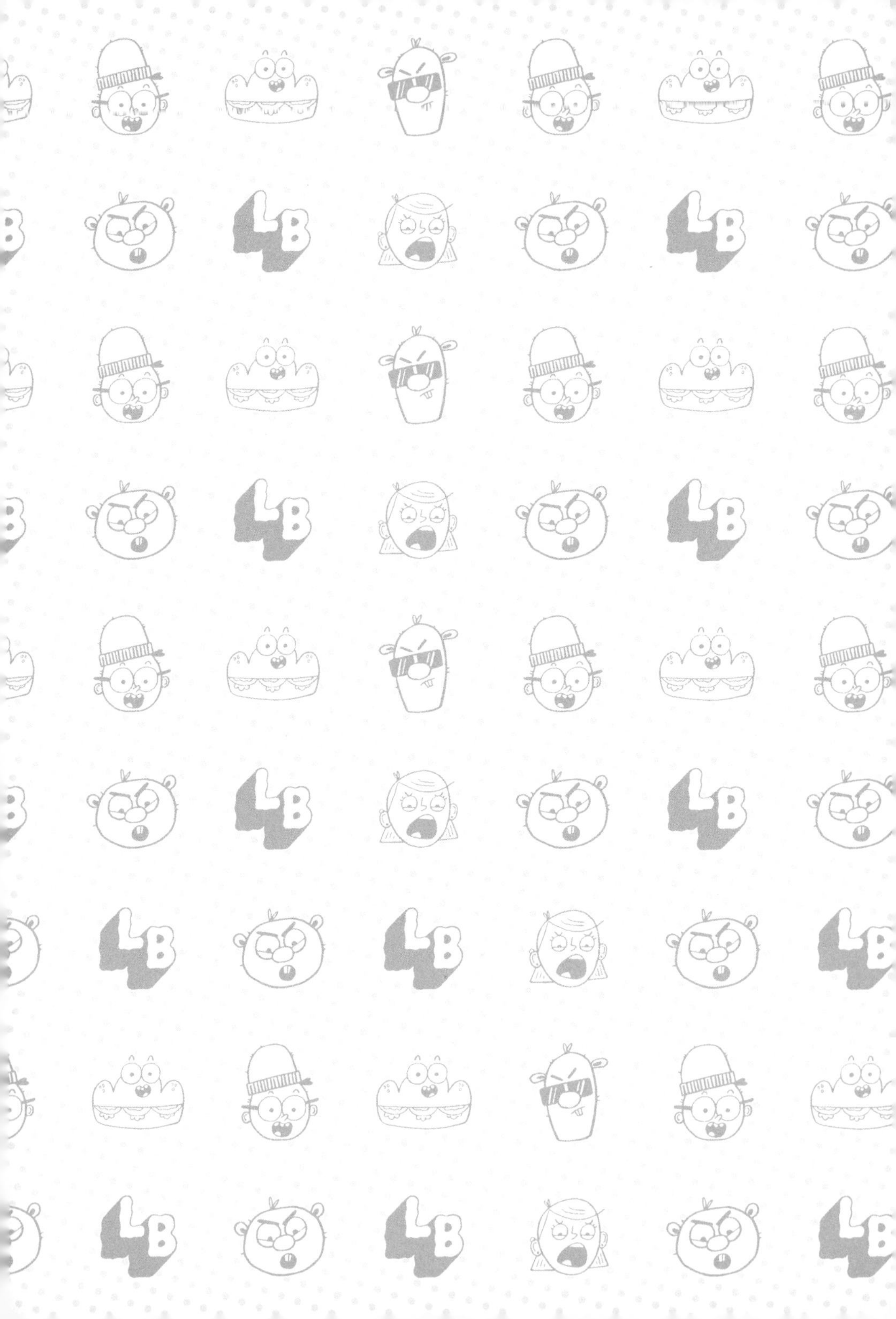